W9-CDM-863

Wrong Place Wrong Time

SILK WHITE

Good2Go Publishing

WRONG PLACE WRONG TIME
Written by SILK WHITE
Cover design: Davida Baldwin
Typesetter: Mychea
ISBN: 978-1-943686-47-6

Copyright ©2017 Good2Go Publishing
Published 2017 by Good2Go Publishing
7311 W. Glass Lane • Laveen, AZ 85339
www.good2gopublishing.com
https://twitter.com/good2gobooks
G2G@good2gopublishing.com
www.facebook.com/good2gopublishing
www.instagram.com/good2gopublishing

BOOKS BY THIS AUTHOR

10 Secrets to Publishing Success
Business Is Business
Business Is Business 2
Business Is Business 3
Married To Da Streets
Never Be The Same
Stranded
Sweet Pea's Tough Choices
Tears of a Hustler
Tears of a Hustler 2
Tears of a Hustler 3
Tears of a Hustler 4
Tears of a Hustler 5
Tears of a Hustler 6
Teflon Queen
Teflon Queen 2
Teflon Queen 3
Teflon Queen 4
Teflon Queen 5
Teflon Queen 6
The Serial Cheater
Time Is Money (An Anthony Stone Novel)
48 Hours to Die (An Anthony Stone Novel)
The Vacation (An Anthony Stone Novel)
Wrong Place Wrong Time

WEB SERIES

The Hand I Was Dealt
Now Available On You Tube

Wrong Place Wrong Time
Now Available on YouTube

acknowledgements

To all of you who are reading this, thank you for stepping inside the bookstore, stopping by the library, or downloading a copy of Wrong Place Wrong Time. I hope you have enjoyed this read from top to bottom. My goal is to get better and better with each story. I want to thank everyone for all their love and support. It is definitely appreciated! Now without further ado Ladies and Gentleman, I give you Wrong Place Wrong Time.

$iLK WHiTE

Wrong Place Wrong Time

one

Keyon placed his luggage in the trunk and slammed the trunk shut. From the outside looking in anyone could tell that he either had an attitude or was upset about something. He slid down in the driver's seat and turned and faced the beautiful woman in the passenger seat. "Sabrina, you better talk to that girl before I have to put my hands on her."

"What did Mya do now?" Sabrina asked.

"I told that girl to be ready over an hour ago, and she's still not ready."

"Mya is at that age where she's feeling herself. I'll have a talk with her." Sabrina placed a hand on top of Keyon's hand in an attempt to calm him down. "Don't let this stress you out."

With his free hand Keyon pressed down on the horn repeatedly until finally Mya came slow-walking out the front door toward the car. Mya slid into the backseat and slammed the door harder than she needed to. If Mya wasn't Keyon's child he would have went upside the child's head.

"Nice of you to join us!" Keyon said, looking at his sixteen-year-old daughter through the rearview mirror.

"Why do I have to go anyway?" Mya spat with an attitude. "I'm old enough to stay home by myself."

"It's a family reunion, and you part of the family, right? Then you have to be there," Keyon explained as he pulled out into traffic. He didn't understand why Mya always gave him a problem instead of going with the flow.

Mya sucked her teeth. "I don't even like that side of the family, so I don't understand why y'all are forcing me to go on this stupid trip."

"Listen!" Sabrina snapped. "You're going, and we all going to have a good time, and I don't want to hear nothing else about this. Am I understood?"

"Yes," Mya mumbled.

"The only reason you want to stay is so you can be with that no-good boyfriend of yours, Marcus," Sabrina said. She knew the real reason why Mya was upset about coming on the road trip. Her new boyfriend was the neighborhood knucklehead, a fake thug that went by the name Marcus. Everyone could see he was on the fast track to the grave or the penitentiary—everyone except Mya.

"That's not why I don't want to . . ."

"Shut your mouth!" Sabrina cut Mya off in mid-sentence. "I don't want to hear another peep out of you for the rest of the ride."

two

A black Tahoe coasted down the street at a steady speed. Each window was heavily tinted. On the inside four gunmen occupied the truck, three men and one female. Each gunman had a no-nonsense look on their face as the soft sounds of Marvin Gaye humming through the speakers. The female driver pulled the truck over to the curb and placed it in park. "Ight, let's do this! In and out. No playing around! Go get that money. I'll be right here waiting for y'all."

The leader of the crew, a tall man that went by the name Jesus, pulled his ski mask down over his face and checked the magazine on his machine gun before slamming the clip back into the base of the gun. "I'm the first man in," Jesus began. "Mike, I want you to pull up the rear." Jesus then turned his attention to the loose cannon of the crew. "Tommy, none of that wild cowboy shit tonight!"

"I'm chilling tonight, but anybody act stupid and it's on!" Tommy said with a scary look on his face. The four gunmen were professional thieves who had been working together for a total of three years. Their motto was as long as their victims did as they were told then nobody would get hurt, but the second their rules weren't obeyed anything was likely to happen. Jesus did a good job of leading his crew to the money and keeping everyone out of jail.

"How much money supposed to be up in here anyway?" Tommy asked.

"Enough." Jesus looked at the driver. "Monica, keep this car running," he said as the three gunmen jumped out of the truck and headed toward the house they came to rob.

Monica sat behind the wheel of the truck, with a nervous look on her face. The four of them had done plenty of jobs in the past, but there was something about the rush of it all that always made Monica a little nervous.

Jesus walked up to the front door and shot the lock off. Without warning, Tommy took a step back and came forward with a strong kick that sent the front door crashing in.

Jesus was the first man in. Immediately he spotted a man sitting on the couch reaching for something. Jesus squeezed down on the trigger of his machine gun and watched as the bullets tore through the man's body.

"Everybody down on the floor now!" Tommy yelled as he grabbed a girl, who stood frozen in the middle of the living room like a deer caught in the headlights, by her hair and roughly tossed her down to the floor.

Jesus and Mike kept everyone in the living room at gunpoint while Tommy made his way toward the kitchen. Tommy stormed into the kitchen and found a woman trying to hide behind the counter. "Get your ass up!" Tommy snatched the woman to her feet by her hair. "Where's the money at?"

"I don't know," the woman replied with a frightened look on her face and tears running down her cheeks.

Tommy turned and slapped the woman down to

the floor. "Does it look like I'm playing with you!" he growled.

"I don't know nothing about no money," the woman cried.

Tommy placed his gun to the side of the woman's head. "Last time I'm going to ask you, where's the money?"

"Upstairs," the woman spat as Tommy roughly escorted her upstairs.

Jesus glanced down at his watch. "Two minutes!" he yelled.

"Get up here!" Tommy snarled, roughly slamming the woman up against the wall. "Which room is the money in?"

The woman was so shaken up that she couldn't speak. So instead she just pointed to the room at the end of the hall. Tommy spun and hit the woman across the top of her head with the gun, knocking the woman unconscious. He then quickly made his way toward the room at the end of the hall. When he reached the door, he kicked it open and barged inside.

"Oh shit!" Tommy cursed, stopping in mid-stride. He looked up and saw a woman standing with a shotgun aimed in his direction. Tommy quickly raised his hands in surrender. He started to say something, but before he could get the words out the shotgun barked and the impact from the blast tossed Tommy's body back out into the hallway.

The loud blast immediately grabbed Mike's attention. "You heard that?" Mike asked, looking over at Jesus.

"I got it," Jesus said as he slowly made his way upstairs. He cautiously let the barrel of his machine gun lead the way. Jesus reached the top of the steps, and the first thing he saw was the first woman lying on the floor unconscious with blood leaking from her head. Jesus looked down the hall and spotted Tommy sprawled out on the floor with a gaping hole in his chest and blood everywhere.

"Don't fuck with me!" a woman's voice boomed, coming from the room at the end of the hall. "I have plenty more bullets, and I'm not afraid to use them!"

Jesus slowly inched his way toward the room at

the end of the hall. He took a deep breath and stuck his arm inside the bedroom, pressed down on the trigger, and blindly filled the room with bullets until he heard the sound of a body hit the floor. Jesus slowly entered the room and spotted a woman lying dead on the floor with multiple bullet holes in her body. He quickly stepped over the body and proceeded to search the room until he found a duffle bag filled with product. Jesus hastily grabbed the bag and rushed back downstairs. "Come on, we out!" he yelled as he and Mike exited the scene of the crime.

Monica sat behind the wheel of the truck with a nervous look on her face when the passenger and back door came open and Jesus and Mike climbed inside.

"Come on, let's go!" Jesus said in a panicked tone.

Monica asked no questions. She stomped down on the gas causing the engine to roar as the truck picked up speed. "Where's Tommy?"

"He didn't make it," Jesus said, removing his ski mask from his face. "Slow down and drive like you got some sense."

Monica slowed the truck down a bit and looked at Jesus through the rearview mirror. "What happened back there?"

"Things got a little crazy," Jesus replied, looking out the back window to make sure they weren't being followed by any cops. "Take us somewhere low key so we can count up this money and regroup."

"We looking real good over here." Mike smiled as he thumbed through a few of the bills that rested in the duffle bag. For the rest of the ride the trio rode in silence. Each person stuck in their own personal thoughts. Thirty minutes later Monica pulled the truck into a rundown Motel 6 parking lot.

"Is this spot low key enough for you?" Monica asked.

"It's perfect," Jesus said as the trio stepped out of the vehicle. "You two go check in while I go get rid of this truck."

"Be careful," Monica said as she watched Jesus get behind the wheel of the truck and pull recklessly out of the parking lot.

Mike and Monica entered their room and looked around with sour looks on their faces. The room looked dingy and old. "Damn, with all the money we making, Jesus couldn't have picked a better place for us to crash?" Mike flopped down on the bed.

"You know Jesus likes for us to be low key," Monica told him. "I'm sure we won't be here too long."

"I hope not."

three

Jesus parked the stolen truck on the side of the road and wiped it down carefully, making sure there weren't any prints left behind. He cautiously looked over both shoulders as he walked a few blocks down, where he flagged down a cab. Jesus slid in the backseat of the cab and gave the cab driver the address he was heading to, when he felt his phone vibrating in his pocket. Jesus removed his phone from his pocket and saw Omar's name flashing across the screen. "Hello?" Jesus answered.

"Do you have some good news for me?" Omar said, cutting straight to the chase.

"We just hit a lick today," Jesus said. "From the looks of it we came off with about $30,000."

"$30,000?" Omar repeated. From the tone of his voice Jesus could tell that Omar was unmoved by the number. "Jesus, do I need to remind you that you and your crew owe me a million dollars?"

"Omar, me and my team doing our best to get that money to you," Jesus assured him. A few months ago Jesus and his crew robbed a stash house. They got away with $60,000, and Tommy killed two people in the process. Little did they know, but the stash house they robbed belonged to a man named Omar, the biggest gangsta New York City had seen in the last twenty years. When Omar found out what had happened he personally paid Jesus and his crew a visit and gave them an ultimatum. The choices were easy: either Jesus and his crew could pay Omar a million dollars, or Omar would have them and their entire families murdered. Without thinking twice Jesus and his crew agreed to pay the million dollars, and since Omar was in a good mood, he gave Jesus and his crew three months to come up with the money.

"Your time is almost out," Omar reminded him.

"We still have thirty days left to get you all your money," Jesus said. So far they had paid Omar $300k.

"Indeed you do, and I pray you and your team

come up with that money." Omar let out an evil laugh. "I'll be in touch." He ended the call, disrespectfully hanging up in Jesus's ear.

four

Sabrina sat in the passenger seat reading an article on her iPhone, when she noticed the car swerve a bit. She looked over to her left and saw Keyon struggling to keep his eyes open. "Baby, why don't you pull over and let me drive for a while," Sabrina suggested.

"I'm fine, baby," Keyon told her. His mouth said that he was fine, but his eyes and body language said he needed to rest.

"Baby, you're not fine. You were just nodding off," Sabrina pointed out. "Pull over so I can help you with the driving."

"Baby, I'm fine," Keyon protested. He refused to let Sabrina drive because he had promised her that she wouldn't have to lift a finger this entire weekend, and didn't want to break his word.

"I saw you nodding off too," Mya added her two cents from the backseat. "Let Mommy drive so we can make it back in one piece."

"You two need to relax," Keyon said in a calm tone. "I got this."

Sabrina went to say something, but kept quiet when she heard Mya's phone ringing from the backseat, so she could eavesdrop.

"Hello?" Mya answered as her face lit up like a Christmas tree, which could only mean that her no-good boyfriend, Marcus, was on the other line. "I miss you too, baby . . . No, I had to go on a stupid road trip with my parents . . . Of course I would have loved to stay with you, but I didn't have no choice," Mya whispered. "Baby, my mother is being nosey, so I'll call you later when I have some privacy . . . I love you too."

"What you know about love?" Sabrina challenged. She hated the fact that her daughter was trying to grow up so fast, but with how all the young kids were wilding nowadays, Sabrina was happy that Mya wasn't pregnant or addicted to any drugs.

"Why are you always trying to be in my business?" Mya sucked her teeth.

"As long as you are under my roof, your business

is my business," Sabrina said as she felt the car swerve again. "Keyon!" she yelled, causing him to jump. "Baby, you're going to get us killed! Please pull over. There's a motel right there."

"I'm good, baby," Keyon yawned.

"No, you're not. Now pull over. We're getting a room," Sabrina stated plainly. Keyon pulled the vehicle into the Motel 6 parking lot and then placed the gear in park.

"I'll be back in a second." Keyon stepped out of the car and entered the office of the Motel 6.

"I'm not staying here. This place is a dump!" Mya complained.

"Hush your mouth right now!" Sabrina snapped. "All you've been doing this whole trip is complaining."

***

Keyon and his family entered the small room, and he quickly kicked off his shoes and flopped down on the bed.

"Get you some rest, baby. I'll be right back. I'm

going to take this girl to get some food." Sabrina grabbed the keys off the table. "Come on!" Sabrina huffed as she and Mya exited the room. As they walked back to the car, they passed a tall man with long dreadlocks. There was something strange about how the man looked at Sabrina, but she brushed it off as the man trying to figure out if she and Mya were prostitutes, since they were staying in such a sleazy motel. Sabrina ignored the tall man and proceeded on to their car.

five

esus stepped into the room and placed his long locks in a loose ponytail. "I got rid of the truck." He sat down on the bed next to Monica. "But now we have a bigger problem. Omar called me, and he wants his money. I tried to get an extension, but he wasn't hearing it."

"So what are we going to do now?" Monica asked.

"I don't know." Jesus shook his head. "I have to think for a second.

"Jesus, we always move as a unit of four, and now with Tommy dead, what are we supposed to do?" Monica asked with a worried look on her face. She knew what would happen to them if they didn't come up with Omar's money.

"Fuck that. We may just have to pull these jobs off with just the three of us," Mike suggested. "Because I'm not sitting around waiting for Omar to kill us."

"I told you I would figure it out. I just need a minute to think," Jesus fumed.

"Damn, what you want, a pillow and blanket to help you think?" Mike said sarcastically. Jesus quickly shot to his feet. His first thought was to put his hands on Mike, but Monica quickly stepped in between the two.

"Calm down, we're all on the same team," she reminded the two. "Instead of fighting amongst ourselves we need to put our heads together and came up with a plan that's going to help us get out of this jam."

"As I was making my way to the room from dropping off the truck I saw two young ladies coming out of the room next door," Jesus began. "I'm not certain if there's a man in the room or not, but I say it's worth a try."

"So what are you saying?" Monica asked, looking a bit confused.

"We go and bum-rush the room, and if there's a boyfriend or husband in the room, we hold his family hostage and make the boyfriend or husband come with us on a few jobs," Jesus said as if he had it all figured out.

"I don't know about that." Mike shook his head. "I'm not sure if I'm willing to put my life in the hands of a stranger."

"Any of y'all have a better idea?" Jesus looked around. "If we don't come up with Omar's money, we're dead. We don't have nothing to lose if you ask me." It was either they take a chance with the strangers next door or deal with Omar. To Jesus the choice was a no-brainer.

"I'm in," Monica announced.

"Come on, let's get this over with," Mike said. He wasn't feeling the idea, but what other choices did they have?

six

*K*eyon lay on the bed asleep when the front door being opened caused his eyes to snap open on reflex. He had dozed off while watching SportsCenter. Sabrina walked in the room with a nice-sized bag of Popeyes in her hand. "Hey, baby, your daughter has something she wants to tell you." She turned and faced Mya.

"I'm sorry about my attitude, and from here on out I'll be on my best behavior," Mya said. While in the car, Sabrina had scolded Mya about her ugly attitude and reminded her how hard her father worked so the both of them could have the nicer things in life.

"It's okay, baby." Keyon sat up on the bed. "Come give me a hug." The two enjoyed a nice tight hug, when they heard a knock at the door. "Who's that?"

Sabrina shrugged. "I don't know." She stood and walked toward the door and opened it. On the other side of the door, Sabrina saw the tall man with the dreads that her and Mya had passed earlier on the way out. "Hi, may I help you?"

"My car won't start. I was wondering if you could give me a jump?" Jesus asked politely.

"No, I'm sorry, I can't help you." As Sabrina went to close the door, the tall man pushed his way inside and jammed a gun in her face.

"If you and your family want to live, then you better do exactly what the fuck I say!" Jesus growled, then roughly shoved Sabrina down to the floor.

seven

"What the hell do you want?" Keyon said, pulling Sabrina and Mya behind him in an attempt to protect them.

"Calm down and nobody has to get hurt," Jesus said in a calm tone as he opened the front door, allowing Monica and Mike to join the party.

"We don't have any money," Keyon volunteered, hoping that would get the dangerous-looking trio to leave him and his family alone.

"I don't want your money. I'm a businessman, so I'm here to negotiate," Jesus said, with his gun aimed at Keyon's face. "Me and my partners here have a few robberies lined up, and we need you to help us pull 'em off!"

"Why me?" Keyon asked with a confused look on his face. He didn't understand why he and his family were being targeted.

"Nothing personal, you just at the wrong place at the wrong time," Jesus told him.

"What happens if I refuse?"

"Then I kill you and your family right now. The choice is yours." Jesus took an aggressive step forward.

"Can I get a second to talk it over with my family real quick?" Keyon asked.

"You got five minutes!"

Keyon huddled in the corner with his family. "I don't know who these people are, but they look dangerous."

"I don't want you to go with those men. You're going to get killed," Sabrina said, with fear written all over her face.

"I don't have a choice. If I don't do it, they saying they going to kill us all," Keyon said.

"Daddy, I don't want you to die," Mya whispered.

"I'm not going to die, baby," Keyon whispered back. At this moment he was willing to say anything to keep his family calm. "He said it was only a few jobs."

"A few jobs?" Sabrina echoed. "Are you crazy,

25

Keyon? You're not a gangster. You have a master's degree, and you've never even touched a gun before in your life," she pointed out. "This is crazy. You're going to get yourself killed, and then they're going to kill us."

"Alright, time's up!" Jesus barked. "What's it going to be?"

"How many jobs we talking?" Keyon asked.

"Four at most."

"Okay, four jobs, and me and my family are free to go," Keyon accepted the terms. Normally he would have never agreed to such crazy job, but this was no normal situation. "Take me on the jobs and let my family go."

"Your family stays here until the jobs are done. Take it or leave it," Jesus spat.

"Come on, let's just get this over with." Keyon hugged his family one last time.

Jesus pulled Monica to the side and began to talk in a low whisper. "Me and Mike going to take this guy out with us so we can get this money," he began. "Keep a close eye on the wife and daughter. If they try anything funny I want you to blow their heads off."

"Not a problem," Monica said as she hugged Jesus and Mike and then watched as the three men exited the room to go handle their business.

eight

Keyon slid in the backseat with Jesus as Mike pulled away from the curb in the freshly stolen truck. "So how does this work?"

"I got an inside tip on a card game that's taking place tonight," Jesus said, looking Keyon in his eyes. "We going to go in there, get that money, then leave. If anyone act stupid, do what you gotta do." He handed Keyon a handgun. "You know how to use that?"

Keyon shook his head no. Jesus quickly snatched the gun from Keyon's hand and showed him how to operate the firearm. "If somebody gives you any trouble you better put a bullet in their face!"

"I got it," Keyon said with a defeated look on his face. There was no way he had the heart or guts to shoot someone in the face, but there was no way he could tell Jesus that.

***

Sabrina and Mya sat on the bed held at gunpoint. A million thoughts ran through Sabrina's mind. Not only were she and her daughter being held at gunpoint, but she also had no idea if her husband was dead or alive. "Why don't you do the right thing and let us go?"

"Doing the right thing is getting this money so we all can stay alive," Monica told her.

"Why don't you get a real job like the rest of us?" Sabrina rolled her eyes. She never understood how people would rather take or steal from another person who goes to work every day instead of going out and getting a job themselves.

"My job is to babysit you two," Monica countered. "Now as long as you two don't do nothing stupid, then I won't have to shoot nobody."

With that being said Sabrina lay down and stared up at the ceiling. She said a silent prayer to the man up above because at a time like this Sabrina and her family were in desperate need of a miracl

nine

*M*ike pulled the stolen truck up across the street from the house the card game was being held at and killed the engine.

"You ready to do this?" Jesus slammed the clip into the base of his machine gun and cocked it back.

Keyon nodded his head. He didn't have any choice but to be ready. There was no turning back at this point. The trio exited the truck and made their way to the front of the house. Without warning, Jesus lifted his foot and kicked the front door. It took three strong kicks before the door finally flew open. Jesus, Mike, and Keyon stormed inside the house and spotted several men sitting around a table that was covered in cards and cash.

"Nobody move!" Jesus yelled as he grabbed the closest man to him, snatched him out of his chair, and slammed him face-first down to the floor. Jesus pulled a pillow case from his back pocket and handed it to Keyon. "Here, fill that up!"

Keyon took the pillow case and made his rounds. He relieved each man of their jewelry, wallets, and anything of value. Keyon reached the last man at the table and removed his wallet, and then his watch from his wrist. He went for the man's ring, when the man quickly pulled his hand back.

"Please don't take my ring," the man pleaded. "This is the last thing my wife gave me before she passed away."

Keyon was about to let the man slide and allow him to keep his wedding ring, when out of nowhere Jesus violently cracked his machine gun over the man's head, causing him to fall out of his chair down to the floor. Before the man could even say a word, Jesus had raised his foot and violently stomped the man's face into the floor then roughly removed the wedding ring from the man's hand.

Once they had everything they needed, the trio made their exit. Keyon ran and jumped in the backseat as Mike stomped down on the gas, making the truck come to life. "Shit wasn't as bad as you thought it would be, was it?" Mike peeked at Keyon

31

through the rearview mirror with smirk on his face.

Keyon removed the ski mask from his face. "I just want to get these jobs over with so me and my family can go free."

"One down, a few more to go," Jesus said with a straight face.

***

Monica sat in a chair. Her feet were propped up on the small table that rested in the corner of the room, all while keeping her gun trained on Sabrina and her daughter. Monica could feel the tension in the air, but she could care less. Monica was there to do a job, and she didn't care who didn't like it.

Seconds later the front door opened and the men entered the room. Sabrina quickly shot to her feet and hugged Keyon tightly. She then began to Pat down his body looking for any wounds.

Keyon grabbed Sabrina's hands. "Baby, I'm fine."

"We were so worried about you," Sabrina expressed. Everything just felt better when Keyon was around, and most importantly things felt safe.

"How did the new jack do?" Monica asked.

"Better than expected," Jesus said as the ringing of his cell phone startled everyone in the room. Jesus pulled his phone out of his pocket and saw Omar's name flashing across the screen. "Hello?"

"You got some good news for me?" Omar asked, not beating around the bush.

"Still working on it as we speak," Jesus replied.

"I don't think you understand what's riding on the line here," Omar said in a serious tone. "If I don't get my money, all you motherfuckers are dead!"

Jesus looked down at the phone as the line went dead.

"What he say?" Mike asked.

"He said if we don't hurry up and get his money we all dead." Jesus helped himself to a seat on the floor. Now he needed to sit and collect his thoughts. Jesus tried to keep a positive attitude, but that was a difficult task when all of their lives were on the line. Monica sat down on the floor beside Jesus.

"Everything is going to be fine," Monica said in a tone just above a whisper. "We going to get Omar his money, and then things will go back to normal."

ten

The next day Jesus sat staring blankly out the Motel room window. After speaking with Omar last night, he knew that he and the crew were going to have to step it up a notch. The fact that he owed someone didn't sit well with Jesus. He was a boss and liked to make his own rules. Having someone on his back was starting to become a huge annoyance.

"What's on your mind?" Monica walked up to Jesus from behind. "You don't seem like yourself."

"This Omar thing isn't sitting too well with me," Jesus admitted. "It's like a dark cloud hanging over all of our heads."

"Don't worry about Omar," Monica said. "We going to pay him his money. Then we never have to be bothered with him again."

"Look after the women. Me and the guys about to head out," Jesus told her. He then walked over toward the bed that Keyon and his family lay on and gave it a hard kick. "Get up. It's time to go."

Keyon got up, hugged his wife, and then followed the gunmen out the door.

***

Keyon sat in the backseat of the stolen truck staring down at the gun on his lap. He silently wondered what he had done so bad in life to deserve to be put in such a sticky situation like this. Here he was in the backseat of a stolen truck about to commit a crime while his wife and daughter were back at the motel being held at gunpoint.

"Hey, new guy!" Jesus barked, snapping Keyon out of his thoughts. "When we get in here it's going to be real loud. If anyone even moves the wrong way, you know what to do."

"Yeah, I know. Shoot them in the face," Keyon said sarcastically.

Mike parked the stolen truck across the street from a rundown looking bar. "Okay, we're here." Mike began loading his weapon. "In and out like always." The trio stepped out of the truck. Their faces were covered in ski masks, and in each of their hands was an automatic weapon.

Jesus was the first man in the bar. "Everybody down on the floor!" He fired three rounds up into the ceiling causing everyone to hit the floor in a panic. Mike quickly hopped over the counter and pistol-whipped both a man and woman who stood behind the bar serving drinks. He then made his way straight to the cash register.

"Nobody fucking move!" Jesus barked. He then turned toward Keyon. "New guy, go do your thing!"

With that said, Keyon began making his rounds removing all the hostages of all their belongings. Keyon felt bad about robbing all the innocent people in the bar, but what choice did he have?

As he removed the valuables of an elderly woman, Keyon noticed the man lying next to her reaching in his waist for something. "Don't even think about it!" Keyon trained his gun on the man. The man's hand froze on the handle of his gun. "Listen, man, I'm a cop, and I'm off duty," he began. "I can't allow y'all to rob this place," he said in a strong whisper.

"Slowly remove your hand from your waist," Keyon said as his hand began to shake a bit.

"I can't do that," the off-duty officer countered with a no-nonsense look in his eyes. The off-duty officer quickly pulled his gun from his holster, leaving Keyon no choice. Keyon closed his eyes and fired three rounds into the officer's chest.

When Jesus heard the shots ring out he quickly headed over in Keyon's direction. "Good work!" he said to Keyon as he fired a round of his own into the officer's already dead body. "Come on, we have to go!"

The trio exited the bar running full speed to the getaway truck. Mike hopped behind the wheel and stomped down on the gas pedal.

"I can't believe I just killed a man," Keyon said in a low tone as he stared blankly out the window. "An off-duty police officer, at that."

"You did a good thing back there," Jesus tried to encourage him. "You saved all of our asses. You a hero!"

"Yeah, I hear you," Keyon mumbled. The truth was he didn't feel like a hero, but instead he felt more like a murderer, a criminal, and a barbarian. He silently wondered what Sabrina and Mya would think of him when they found out what he had done.

"What you over there thinking about?" Jesus asked, peeking over at Keyon.

"I just killed a man!" Keyon snapped. "I didn't sign up for this, man. You told me all I had to do was help out and assist you guys!"

Mike looked at Jesus through the rearview mirror, and Jesus gave him a silent nod. Mike then quickly pulled the truck over to the side of the road. Jesus stepped out of the backseat and walked around the back of the truck. He opened Keyon's door and snatched him out of the backseat.

"Listen, motherfucker!" Jesus barked as he jammed his gun to the side of Keyon's head. "We almost at the finish line. Don't go start bitching up on me now!" he yelled. "Now you did what you had to do back there. Get back in the car and keep your mouth shut."

Keyon got back in the truck with an aggravated look on his face. He hated the fact that someone else had control over his life at the moment. He badly wanted to tell Jesus to kiss his ass, but he knew doing something like that may cost him and his family their life. After about a twenty-minute ride, Keyon noticed the truck pull up in front of a nice expensive-looking house. "Who lives here?"

"You ask too many questions!" Mike pulled his ski mask down over his face and stepped out of the truck. The trio slowly crept toward the back entrance of the house. Jesus pulled a silenced handgun from a small bag and shot the lock off the door. He then came forward with his shoulder and busted the door open. Jesus and the crew entered through the basement and hit the lights.

"You two wait down here while I go check out the house," Jesus said as he silently roamed through the house. Jesus slowly crept up the stairs with a strong two-handed grip on his silenced weapon. The closer he got to the top of the stairs, the more he could hear what sounded like a woman talking on the phone. Jesus peeked around the corner and spotted a woman talking on the phone while cleaning the kitchen. He slowly crept around the corner, threw the woman in a chokehold with one arm, and placed his gun to her head with the other hand. "Hang up the phone!" Jesus growled in a strong whisper, then roughly escorted the woman down to the basement. Once in the basement, Jesus violently slapped the woman down to the floor.

"Where's the money?" Jesus asked in a calm tone.

"What money?" the woman said, faking ignorance. Word got back to Jesus that this home was the stash house of one of the biggest drug dealers from the Bronx, and he refused to leave the house empty-handed.

"If I have to ask you again it's going to get real ugly in here!" Jesus threatened the woman.

"I don't know what money you talking about," the woman lied.

Jesus responded by slapping the woman back down to the floor. "New guy, watch this chick, and don't let her out of your site while we go search the house," Jesus said as he and Mike exited the basement to go search the rest of the home for all the money he had heard was inside.

Jesus and Mike tore through the house like a hurricane looking for money and product. The two would have been happy to find one or the other, but if they could somehow come away with both, that would be even better.

Mike entered the master bedroom and flipped the mattress searching for the jackpot. He knew if they didn't find nothing, things wouldn't end well for the woman in the basement. Mike wasn't into hurting women or children, but with the stakes being so high he was willing to turn a blind eye this one time.

Jesus entered another bedroom and removed each drawer from the dresser one by one, dumping all of the content onto the floor. The more he searched the house and came up emptyhanded, the angrier he became.

***

Down in the basement Keyon stood sweating bullets as he held the woman at gunpoint. His adrenaline mixed with the heat from the ski mask wrapped tightly around his face turned him into a sweaty mess. Keyon's mind raced a hundred miles a minute as he stood there in the basement. He could hear what sounded like furniture being moved coming from upstairs. Keyon didn't know what was going on up there, but whatever it was it couldn't be anything good.

"Oh hell no!" The woman shot to her feet and began making her way toward the door that led upstairs.

"Not another step!" Keyon stepped in the woman's path, blocking her entrance through the door.

"Are you crazy? You hear them up there breaking up all my shit!" the woman snapped.

"Listen, please go back and sit down," Keyon pleaded.

"Fuck you!" the woman spat. "If you were going to shoot me, you would have shot me already," the woman said as she tried to brush by the gunman.

Keyon spun and hit the woman over the head with his gun, dropping her where she stood. Keyon then stood over the woman and began to hit her in the face repeatedly with the gun. "I told you not to move . . . I begged you . . . Now look what you made me do!" Keyon finally snapped out of his trance and looked down at the bloody woman and stood frozen in shock for a moment. His actions were animalistic, and the sight of the unconscious woman didn't sit well with him. Keyon was turning into a monster right before his own eyes. Only an animal would do such a horrible thing to a woman. Keyon tried to justify his action by telling himself he violently attacked that woman to protect his family, but the truth was he attacked that woman because she showed a little bit of resistance. He could have easily wrestled the woman down to the floor and contained her, but instead he decided to take the savage route. "Lord, please forgive me," Keyon said as a quick prayer as the noise coming from upstairs grew louder.

Upstairs Mike searched through a closet and came across two large duffle bags. He quickly peeked inside, and smiled when he saw nothing but dead presidents staring back at him. "Jackpot!" Mike yelled with excitement.

Jesus quickly entered the room. "We good?"

"No, we're great!" Mike announced as the two men quickly made their way back to the basement. Jesus stepped foot in the basement, and the first thing he saw was the woman laid out on the floor in a pool of her own blood.

Jesus's eyes went from the bloody woman back up to Keyon. "Come on, we have to go!" he ordered as the trio exited the house and jogged back toward the stolen getaway truck.

For the entire ride back to the hotel room Keyon sat with his head back and his eyes closed. He still couldn't believe the vicious act that he had committed on that woman back there. Keyon had never put his hands on a woman in his life. All he could think about was what if that woman was his mother, his sister, or better yet, his wife.

"You good?" Jesus asked. He could tell that something was bothering Keyon.

"I got a lot on my mind," Keyon responded in a defeated tone.

"I know this has been a lot for you and your family. I just want you to know that I'm here if you ever want to talk," Jesus offered.

"I don't mean no disrespect, but I really don't feel like talking right now. I have a lot to think about," Keyon said as a tear managed to fall from his eye.

eleven

Sabrina lay on the hard motel mattress, staring up at the ceiling while Mya lay snuggled up on her chest sleeping peacefully. There was no way Sabrina would be able to sleep at a time like this. She was hungry and had no idea if her husband was dead or alive. All Sabrina wanted to do was go home, but unfortunately her nightmare was far from being over. Sabrina had said several prayers, but here she was still trapped in the motel room, being held at gunpoint. "Everything is going to be okay," she kept telling herself over and over again, hoping she could somehow speak her words into existence. A loud snoring sound snapped Sabrina out of her negative thoughts. At first she thought the snoring was coming from Mya, until she heard the sound again and realized that it wasn't coming from her daughter but instead from Monica. Sabrina slowly sat up and watched the gunwoman carefully for about two minutes, just to make sure her eyes weren't playing tricks on her. There Monica sat with her head slowly bobbing back and forth with her mouth open. Sabrina watched Monica sleep for a few more seconds before she decided this was her chance to escape. She gently tapped Mya awake.

"Mya, wake up!" Sabrina whispered as she watched Mya stir. "Wake up!"

Mya went to say something, when she felt her mother's hand clamp down over her mouth.

"Shhhh," Sabrina said with a finger held up to her lips. "Look!" She nodded over toward Monica. Mya looked over in Monica's direction. When she saw the woman was sleep she already knew what her mother was thinking.

"No!" Mya said with a scared look on her face. "What if she wakes up?"

"This may be our only chance to escape!" Sabrina whispered. "Stop being scared and come on!"

Sabrina and Mya quietly eased off the bed and crept toward the door. Sabrina knew what they were doing was dangerous, but this was their only chance at freedom. The only way to get to the front door was to walk past Monica, who was sleeping with her gun still in her hand. Sabrina gave Mya a slight shove in the back to get her feet moving in the right direction. Mya slowly tiptoed past Monica and reached the door, where she then waved her mother over.

Sabrina took a deep breath and then began tiptoeing toward the door, when Monica's eyes shot open.

"Bitch!" Monica growled as she shot up from the chair and tackled Sabrina down to the bed and slapped her across the face with the gun.

"Mya, run!" Sabrina yelled as she felt warm blood running down her face. Mya stood frozen. A part of her wanted to help her mother, while the other part of her was scared to death. "Run!" Sabrina yelled as she saw Monica aim her gun in Mya's direction. Instantly Sabrina's motherly instincts kicked in. She jumped off the bed and grabbed the wrist that Monica held the gun in. While the two women fought over the gun, Mya quickly ran out the front door and never looked back.

"Bitch!" Monica punched Sabrina in the face and then regained control of her gun and aimed it at Sabrina's head. "Move again, and I'll shoot you in the face!" Monica threatened. She removed a roll of duct tape from her bag and quickly taped Sabrina's hands behind her back and shoved her face-first down to the floor. Once that was done Monica quickly ran out of the motel room to see if she saw Mya anywhere, but she had no luck.

Monica walked back over to Sabrina, who lay on the floor looking up at her. "Bitch!" Monica kicked Sabrina in the pit of her stomach. "Now you and your family is going to die!" Monica raised her leg and stomped Sabrina's head down into the floor.

"I'm sorry!" Sabrina cried. She was willing to say anything to get the woman to stop kicking her.

"Oh, now you sorry?" Monica grabbed a hand full of Sabrina's hair and punched her in the face. Monica was about to stomp Sabrina's head into the floor again, but paused when they both heard a forceful knock at the door. Monica swiftly kneeled down and placed her gun to Sabrina's head. "You

make a sound and your whole family is dead!"
Monica threatened as she stood up and walked over
to the door. "Who is it?" she sang in a friendly voice.

"Police!" the voice on the other end of the door
replied.

"One second," Monica called out as she quickly
ran back over to Sabrina and cut the duct tape from
around her wrists. "You do or say anything to tip the
cops off, and your family is dead."

Monica walked back to the door, placed her gun
into her waistband at the small of her back, and then
cracked the door just enough so the officer could see
her eyes. "Hi, can I help you?"

"Yes, I got a call about a noise complaint. Is
everything alright in there?" the officer asked with a
raised brow.

"Yes, everything is fine. You sure you have the
right room?" Monica faked ignorance.

"This is room 204 right?" The officer looked at
the number on the door to confirm he had the right
room.

"Well, officer, sorry I couldn't be of any help."

Monica went to close the door, but the officer quickly stuck his boot in the door before it could shut.

"Mind if I come inside and take a look?" the officer asked.

"Sure, of course." Monica stepped to the side and allowed the officer inside. The officer stepped foot inside the room and looked around. His eyes landed on Sabrina, and Sabrina gave the officer a nice friendly smile.

"You ladies keep the noise down." The officer tipped his hat and then made his exit.

twelve

*M*ya stood on the corner with a scared and nervous look on her face. She was happy she had been able to escape from the motel room, but she feared for her mother. Mya hoped and prayed that the gunwoman didn't murder her mother or injure her too badly. Every few seconds Mya found herself looking over her shoulder for trouble. For the first time in her life Mya was without her mother and father, and she was scared to death. An all-black car pulled up to the curb where Mya stood. The passenger window rolled down, and Mya's boyfriend, Marcus, yelled, "Come on, baby, get in!"

When Mya heard Marcus's voice, her face lit up. When she escaped the room, the first thing she did was call her boyfriend and tell him to come pick her up. Mya jumped in the passenger seat and gave Marcus the biggest hug.

"What's going on, baby?" Marcus asked with a concerned look on his face. When Mya had called him, she was hysterical and scared out of her mind.

"Some stick-up kids kidnapped me, my mother, and my father," Mya told him. "If we don't save my parents they're going to kill them."

"Baby, don't worry about nothing," Marcus said confidently. "I'mma go round up the homies, and we going to handle this!"

"Thanks, baby, but we have to hurry up before something bad happens to them," Mya said.

"Don't worry, baby, your man is going to handle everything!" Marcus promised her.

***

Mike parked the stolen truck a few blocks away from the motel on a quiet street. The trio exited the truck and began walking back toward the motel.

"How we looking?" Mike asked.

"We still have a long way to go to get Omar all of his money, but these licks we just pulled off definitely help," Jesus answered. "A few more big jobs and we'll be all straight."

Keyon walked down the street keeping to

himself. He was still disappointed in himself for his actions and was trying to think of a way he could somehow rectify the situation.

"You good?" Jesus asked, noticing how quiet Keyon was.

"Yeah, I'm straight," Keyon lied. He really wanted to use the gun he had to kill both Jesus and Mike, but if he did that he knew his wife and daughter would suffer dearly, so for now he just had to continue to go with the flow.

"When this is all over I'm going to throw you and your family a couple of dollars," Jesus told him. "I appreciate all your help."

"I don't need anything from you. I just want to go home," Keyon said honestly. This was a bad nightmare that he was ready to be over with.

"Lighten up, Keyon, everything is going to be alright!" Mike cut in. "You and your family will be free soon!"

Keyon sucked his teeth. "How are you so sure of that? What, I get killed or we all get arrested before it's time for y'all to let me go? Huh? Then what?"

"You worry too much," Mike brushed him off. "Everything is going to be fine."

thirteen

Sabrina stood with the motel phone up to her ear for a few seconds before hanging it up. "No answer."

"Try again!" Monica barked, with her gun pointed at Sabrina.

"My daughter is not answering her phone!" Sabrina snapped with an attitude. She already knew that she and her family were as good as dead, so Sabrina no longer cared what happened to her.

"Try to call her again!" Monica yelled. "Because when the men get back it's going to get ugly!" As soon as the words left Monica's mouth, the front door opened and in walked Jesus followed by Keyon and Mike.

"Where's the girl?" Jesus asked immediately.

"Me and the mother got into a little scuffle, and the girl escaped," Monica answered. "I was going to shoot her, but I didn't want to draw too much attention to the room while y'all were gone."

Jesus turned his attention to Sabrina and pressed his gun into her forehead. "You got to the count of ten to tell where the girl is. One!"

"I don't know where she is," Sabrina said.

"Two!"

"I called her phone ten times and she's not answering," Sabrina said as her eyes began to water.

"Three!"

"Listen, we have to work something out. My wife doesn't know where she is," Keyon cut in. He was trying to figure out a way to buy his family some more time.

"Four!" Jesus continued to count, with an unmoved look on his face.

"Okay, okay, I think I know where we can find her," Keyon said, thinking fast on his toes.

"Where?"

"Okay, it's this guy that Mya talks to named Marcus. I'm sure she ran straight to him." Keyon hoped he was right because if he wasn't, him and his entire family would definitely be shot down like dogs.

"Where can we find this guy Marcus at?" Jesus asked, finally removing the barrel of his gun from Sabrina's forehead.

"I can take you to where he hangs out at," Keyon said as the trio exited the room in search for Marcus and Mya.

***

Mya sat in the passenger seat of Marcus's car with a worried look on her face. "What's taking so long?"

"Patience, baby," Marcus said in a calm tone as Rick Ross's voice hummed through the car's speakers at a low volume. "The homies are on the way. As soon as they get here we going to go take care of those fake stick-up kids."

"We need to go now!" Mya pressed the issue. "My family could be getting murdered right now."

"Baby, just relax. Your man's going to handle everything," Marcus promised.

fourteen

K eyon sat in the back of the stolen truck and said a silent prayer. He knew the men who he shared a car with were dangerous and had no regard for human life.

"How much further?" Mike asked in an agitated tone.

"Make a right at the light," Keyon said from the backseat. The truck was getting closer and closer to the destination, and he feared the outcome when everything was all said and done. "Make a left right here and slow down," Keyon instructed. He could now see Marcus's car in his line of vision. "Okay, there's his car right there."

Once the car came to a stop, Jesus quickly opened his door and was about to step out, when Keyon grabbed his arm.

"That's my daughter. Please let me handle this," Keyon begged.

"Handle your business!" Jesus said as he and

Keyon exited the truck and made a beeline for Marcus's car.

Keyon walked up to the passenger door of the car and snatched Mya out. "What the hell is wrong with you!" he scolded her. "What the hell were you thinking? You could have gotten us all killed!"

"I was just trying to survive, Daddy. I'm sorry." Mya buried her head in her father's chest as tears streamed down her face.

On the other side of the car Jesus roughly snatched Marcus out of the driver's seat and slapped the taste out of his mouth. "You think you tough?" Jesus snarled. He flung Marcus against the wall and then delivered a hard knee to Marcus's stomach, causing him to double over in pain.

"I'm sorry," Marcus said, looking up at the crazed man with dreads. All he was trying to do was help his girlfriend get out of a jam. He had no idea things would end up going this far. "Please don't kill me," he begged. Marcus was rewarded with the butt of the gun to the side of his head.

"Shut up!" Jesus growled as he aimed his gun at

Marcus's head. "Keyon, come take care of this!"

"Take care of it how? You already beat him up," Keyon said with a confused look on his face.

"If you and your family want to live, then you better shoot this scumbag in his face!" Jesus held out the gun.

Having no other choice, Keyon slowly took the gun out of Jesus's hand and aimed it at Marcus's face.

"Please, man, you don't have to do this," Marcus said, pleading for his life. He placed his palms together in a praying motion and continued to beg. "I promise you won't hear from or see me ever again."

Keyon's eyes began to water as he continued to aim the gun at the young man's face. The more he looked into Marcus's eyes, the more he realized that Marcus was just a kid, a kid who thought he was grown.

"Daddy, no!" Mya ran toward her father, but Jesus quickly grabbed her by the waist and restrained her. Mya struggled and fought to free herself from Jesus's grip, but it was no use. "No, Daddy, please don't do it. Please, Daddy!"

Keyon stood there with the business end of his gun aimed at Marcus's face. Tears rolled down his cheeks as his hand began to tremble. Once again he found himself in a no-win situation. It was either kill this kid, or him and his whole family were in jeopardy of being executed. Keyon knew the clock was ticking, and had to move fast. Keyon closed his eyes and squeezed the trigger. Marcus's head violently jerked back as the bullet blew half of his face off.

"Nooooo!" Mya screamed as she melted down to her knees. She couldn't believe what she had just witnessed. Her father had just shot her boyfriend dead right in front of her.

"Come on, we gotta go!" Jesus said as he quickly slipped into the passenger seat of the stolen truck.

Keyon quickly tried to help Mya up off the ground, but she began kicking and screaming, drawing a bunch of unneeded attention to them as well as the stolen getaway truck. "Come on, baby, we have to go!" Keyon huffed as he forcefully shoved

Mya into the backseat. Once everyone was inside the truck, Mike pulled away from the curb in a hurry.

The ride back to the motel was a quiet one. Each person was stuck in their own thoughts. Jesus kept peeking at Keyon through the rearview mirror. Jesus knew what he had forced Keyon to do wasn't right, but he had no idea what Mya may have told Marcus about them, and with the stakes so high, he wasn't willing to risk it. The wrong thing said to the wrong person, and all of them could find themselves behind bars.

Keyon placed his hand on top of Mya's hand. "Baby, I'm sorry. I had to do what I had to do."

Mya quickly jerked her hand out of her father's grip. "I hate you!" she spat, with venom dripping from her voice. In Mya's eyes, she no longer had a father.

"Baby, you do know I had no choice, right?" Keyon tried to explain. "I'm sorry," he said with a defeated look on his face. Mya ignored her father and just stared blankly out the window for the remainder of the ride. She did her best to fight back the tears that threatened to run down her face, but Mya could no longer suppress the tears.

Jesus glanced up at the rearview mirror and saw Mya crying her eyes out. Inside he felt a little bad for Keyon and his family. They were just at the wrong place at the wrong time.

fifteen

Sabrina sat on the stiff bed in the motel room with a sour look on her face. She was bored, tired, and hungry—not to mention cranky. Sabrina was sick of being stuck in the small room, and more importantly she was tired of not knowing if her husband and daughter were even alive. Sabrina looked up and noticed Monica typing away on her phone. "Hey, can you text one of your partners and ask them if they found my daughter yet?"

"The men must be busy," Monica replied. "I texted Jesus over an hour ago, and I haven't received a response yet."

"Mind if I ask you a question?" Sabrina asked.

Monica shrugged. "Go ahead."

"How did you get started in such a violent business like this one?" Sabrina asked.

"It's a long story."

"Look around," Sabrina joked. "We don't have nothing but time."

"Well Jesus used to date my sister. Then she died in a car accident," Monica said as her eyes began to get watery. "Jesus has been taking care of me ever since."

"I'm so sorry to hear about your sister," Sabrina said in a sincere tone. She too had lost a family member not too long ago, so she knew exactly what Monica was going through. "So how did you get into the robbery game?"

"Well it came to a point where I got tired of Jesus taking care of me and just giving me money, so I told him I wanted to work for mines," Monica told her. "And I've been a part of the team ever since."

"So how did you feel after you did your first job?" Sabrina asked. Monica's story was very interesting to her and was an example of how one bad decision could change a person's life forever.

"Well, I've never really done a real job," Monica confessed. "All Jesus allows me to do is drive the getaway car. He's very protective over me."

"I think your story is amazing," Sabrina said. She was glad that the two were able to have a peaceful conversation. "Do you think about your sister often?"

At the mention of her sister, Monica's eyes immediately began to water. "I think about her all the time," she said, then burst into tears.

"Aw, don't cry." Sabrina walked over to Monica and began to comfort her. The two women shared a long tight hug. At that moment a friendship was born.

sixteen

*J*esus and the crew walked up the stairs toward the room, when he stopped and grabbed Keyon. "Aye, y'all go on in the room. I have to talk to Keyon in private for a second." Once Mike and Mya were out of earshot Jesus began.

"Hey, you know you did the right thing back there, right?"

"Yeah, killing my daughter's boyfriend was the right thing to do," Keyon said sarcastically. "He was just a kid."

"That 'kid' could have put us all in jail for life," Jesus countered. "You killing that kid protects me as well as your family."

"What am I supposed to do when all of this is over, huh?" Keyon's voice rose a few notches. "My daughter hates me and will never look at me the same."

"Trust me, when this is all over with you're going to be your daughter's hero!" Jesus said with confidence.

"Hmmp," Keyon huffed. "Yeah right."

***

Sabrina was sitting on the bed when she saw the room door open. She jumped off the bed and ran to the door when she saw Mya. "Oh my god, Mya, are you okay?"

"Dad killed him," Mya cried. She had been crying the entire car ride back to the motel. "Dad killed Marcus!"

"Don't worry, baby, everything is going to be okay." Sabrina gently rubbed Mya's back in an attempt to comfort her. "I'm going to talk to your father in private when he gets in. Don't worry, baby, we're going to be okay."

Sabrina led Mya over to the bed and lay her down, all while continuing to gently rub her back. Minutes later Jesus and Keyon entered the room.

Keyon walked in the room and made a beeline straight for the bed, where he flopped down and stared straight up at the ceiling. Keyon's mind was racing a hundred miles per second. He knew the relationship he once had with his daughter was now destroyed and more than likely wouldn't be able to be repaired.

"You okay, baby?" Sabrina asked in a soft voice. She could tell by the look on her husband's face that he wasn't okay. Keyon didn't respond. Instead he continued to stare blankly up at the ceiling while a single tear escaped his eye.

Jesus walked over and sat on the floor, with his back placed up against the wall. He was getting ready to say something to Monica, when he felt his phone vibrating in his pocket. Jesus looked down at his screen and noticed he had just received a text message from Omar: "I need to see you. Meet me at the spot in an hour."

Jesus slipped his phone back down into his pocket and sighed loudly.

"What's wrong?" Monica asked with a look of concern on her face. Lately the stick-up team had been having such bad luck that Monica was already expecting to hear the worst.

"Omar just texted me and said he wants me to meet him at the spot in an hour," Jesus said. The look on his face said it all. Jesus wasn't happy about going to meet up with Omar. A meeting with Omar, and anything was likely to happen.

"He wants to meet with all of us?" Mike asked.

"Nah, just me," Jesus replied.

"Man, I don't trust Omar. What if he's trying to set you up?" Mike asked.

"Yeah, what if he's just trying to lure you out there so he can kill you?" Monica said with a concerned look on her face. No one trusted Omar, and the sudden request had everyone's antennas raised.

"The one thing about Omar is that he loves money," Jesus explained. "If he kills me, then he doesn't get his money." Jesus knew that more than anything Omar was a businessman, so he wasn't too worried about meeting up with him. Jesus stood to his feet, grabbed his gun, and headed toward the door.

"Be careful!" Monica called out as Jesus exited the room.

seventeen

Jesus got behind the wheel of the stolen truck and quickly pulled out into traffic. On his lap rested a snub nose .38, just in case he ran into any trouble, not to mention Jesus needed something if Omar was in fact trying to set him up. For the past twenty-four hours Jesus had been doing some serious thinking, and once he paid Omar back his money he was really considering retiring from the game. Thoughts of starting a new life all over from scratch were looking more and more attractive with each mission. Jesus pulled the stolen truck up to the location that he and Omar always met. He was a bit early, so Jesus decided to step out of the truck and lean on the hood as he pulled a joint from his pocket, placed it between his lips, and then placed fire to the end.

Just as Jesus was finishing the joint, he spotted an all-black navigator pull around the corner at a slow creep. Immediately Jesus knew Omar had arrived. The black truck stopped directly in front of Jesus. Jesus took a last pull on the joint then flicked it as he opened the back door and slid inside.

Omar sat in the backseat dressed in an all-black tailored suit. In his hand was a glass of vodka and orange juice. "Nice of you to make it on such short notice," Omar started off the conversation. "So tell me, what's been going on?"

"Just been out here trying to get you your money," Jesus answered.

"Word on the streets is you lost a man on the job and now you picked up some new jack to help you pull off jobs." Omar sipped his drink. "Is this true?"

"Yeah, how did you know?"

"It's my job to know everything that's going on," Omar said with a straight face. "So tell me, what do you plan on doing with this family once you've paid off your debt?"

Jesus shrugged. "I'm going to let them go." He could tell by how Omar's facial expression changed that he wasn't too happy with his answer.

"Does the family know anything about me?"

Omar asked, staring out the tinted window.

"No, of course not," Jesus answered quickly. The last thing he needed was for Omar to think he was out running his mouth to strangers. "You know I would never tell anyone about our business."

"Once you're done with all these jobs I want you to kill that family." Omar sipped his drink again. "I want you to kill every last one of them and make it messy."

Jesus had already promised Keyon that when all this was over and done with he would release him and his family. Jesus didn't want to kill Keyon and his family, but at the moment all he could say was, "Sure, no problem."

Omar smiled. "I've always liked you, Jesus, you know that? As soon as I met you I knew you were smart and not dumb like the rest of these fools out here."

"Thank you."

"But the real reason I called you out here is because I need a favor," Omar admitted.

"What you need?" Jesus asked curiously. Even if

Jesus didn't want to do Omar a favor at the moment, there was no way he could have said no.

"I need you to pick up a car for me," Omar began. "I'll text you the address where you can find the car. The keys will be on top of the front tire." Omar paused to make sure Jesus was processing all of the information that was being given to him. "When you get inside the car, there will be a paper with an address on it in the glove compartment. I want you to drop the car off at that address."

"What's inside the car?" Jesus asked.

"You ask too many questions!" Omar snapped. "Just make sure you get the car to that address."

Jesus stepped out of the backseat of Omar's truck and watched as his vehicle sped away. Jesus had no clue why Omar wanted him to transport a car to a secret location, but with him being in debt to him, Jesus was in no position to say no.

He pulled away from the curb, and his mind couldn't help but wonder what was in the car that Omar wanted him to transport. Jesus knew until he cleared his debt with Omar he would always be enslaved to him. "I have to hurry up and get this debt paid," Jesus said to himself. Jesus sat still at a red light, and Omar's words replayed in his mind. He still didn't understand why Omar wanted Keyon and his family dead. The problem was Jesus had given Keyon his word to release him and his family once he was done with them. Jesus's focus was interrupted when his phone buzzed notifying him that he had just received a text message. He looked down at his phone and saw that the message was from Monica, asking if he was okay. Jesus parked the stolen truck a few blocks away and then began his hike back toward the motel. When he reached the parking lot of the motel, he noticed a man and a woman outside arguing. At first Jesus was going to ignore the couple, but the closer he got, the louder the man began to yell. Jesus made it halfway up the stairs, when the man backhanded the woman down to the ground. Jesus heard a loud slap, turned around, and saw the woman on the ground holding the side of her face. Without thinking twice Jesus made a U-turn heading in the direction of the couple. Jesus knew if he didn't put an end to the dispute the motel parking lot would be flooded with cops in a matter of minutes, and he couldn't allow that to happen.

"Yo, my man!" Jesus said, grabbing the man's attention. "You going to have to take all that somewhere else."

"Fuck you think you talking to?" the man said aggressively, looking Jesus up and down.

"Fam, you making a lot of noise and causing a disturbance," Jesus said in a calm tone. "Do me a favor and take all that noise inside."

"I'mma tell you like this," the man said, taking an aggressive step toward Jesus. "I suggest you mind your motherfucking business before I do you like I just did this bitch!"

Without warning, Jesus pulled a knife from his back pocket and jammed it in the man's throat, sending a spray of blood everywhere. The woman on the ground fixed her mouth to scream, when Jesus raised his feet and kicked the woman in the face. Jesus then removed his gun from the small of his back and attached a silencer onto the barrel.

"Please don't!" the woman begged, but her cries were ignored. Before the woman got a chance to say another word, Jesus fired two silenced shots into the woman's chest.

PSST! PSST!

Jesus then turned his focus to the tough guy who lay on the ground bleeding, and fired four shots into the man's face.

PSST! PSST! PSST! PSST!

Jesus bent down and removed the car keys from the tough guy's pockets, popped the trunk, and tossed the man's dead body in the trunk. He then turned his attention to the dead woman and struggled to get the body inside the trunk.

"Damn!" Jesus huffed when he saw the woman's legs hanging out of the trunk. Having to move quickly on his feet Jesus walked around to the back door, opened it, and then went back and pulled the woman's body out of the trunk. He then carried it to the backseat, where he tossed it inside and slammed the door shut. Jesus looked around to make sure no one saw the act he had just committed. Once he was sure the coast was clear Jesus walked around the car, got behind the wheel, and pulled out of the parking lot like a madman.

eighteen

*M*ike sat leaned back in his chair while everyone else slept. In his hand was a machine gun. He and Monica had decided to take turns sleeping so the one who was awake could keep an eye on the two hostages. Mike glanced down at his watch when he noticed Monica sit up from her sleep and stretch.

"Jesus ain't made it back yet?" Monica yawned.

Mike shook his head. "He should have been back by now. I hope he's okay."

"I texted him a few hours ago, and I didn't get a reply," Monica said with a worried look on her face. This was why neither she nor Mike wanted Jesus to go meet with Omar alone.

"If I don't hear from Jesus in the next hour I'm going out to look for him," Mike said. As soon as the words left his lips, the front door opened and in walked Jesus.

"Oh my god, we were so worried about you!"

Monica ran and hugged Jesus so tight that she almost suffocated him. "Where have you been?"

"Ran into a little problem," Jesus said as if murdering the couple and hiding their bodies was no big deal.

"What did Omar want?" Mike asked.

"He asked me to go pick up a car for him and drop it off at a secret location."

"You think he may be trying to set you up?" Monica asked with a look of concern on her face.

"I doubt it. If he wanted me dead he could have killed me when I went to meet with him earlier," Jesus explained. He knew whatever was in the car that Omar wanted him to deliver had something to do with some money.

"I'm not letting you go drop that car off alone!" Mike spat. "We work better as a team anyway." Mike knew if something jumped off he would be able to watch Jesus's back and vice versa.

"I'm not going alone," Jesus said. "I'm taking Keyon with me." This caused everyone in the room to look at him like he had lost his mind.

"You bugging!" Mike huffed. "You taking Keyon with you is like you going alone. He's not going to be able to watch your back if something pops off."

"We can't leave Monica here to watch all three of them. Keyon can easily overpower her," Jesus pointed out. "I need you to stay here and help Monica watch these two. I can handle Keyon."

"I trust that you know what you doing." Mike extended his arm and gave Jesus a fist bump.

"Come on, Keyon, you coming with me!" Jesus walked over to the bed and gave it a light kick.

"Be careful." Monica hugged Jesus before he and Keyon walked out the front door.

"I hope Jesus knows what he's doing." Mike looked over at Monica. He didn't trust Omar one bit and couldn't wait until their debt was paid so they could be free and go back to their normal routine. Mike had no faith in Keyon when it came to watching Jesus's back.

"I trust Jesus's judgment." Monica plugged her phone into the outlet on the wall so it could charge.

"Um, excuse me." Sabrina sat up on the bed. "Can I step outside for a second and stretch my legs please?"

"Shut that noise up!" Mike barked. There was no way he was going to allow Sabrina or her daughter to step outside. Mya had messed it up for the both of them.

"I just need a little fresh air," Sabrina continued to press the issue. She was tired of being trapped inside that stupid room. Everyone had gotten a chance to get some fresh air, everyone except her. "Please, you can even step outside with me if you're worried about me trying to run."

"Let the girl get some fresh air, Mike," Monica said. "Go out there with her and keep an eye on her."

Mike sighed loudly as he stood to his feet. "Come on, I ain't got all day!"

Monica shook her head as she watched the two step outside.

nineteen

Sabrina stepped outside and inhaled a lung full of fresh air. It felt good to get out of that stuffy motel room, even if it was only for a second. "So when this is all over, what's the first thing you plan on doing?" Sabrina asked.

"First thing I'm doing is going to see my girlfriend," Mike said, rubbing his hands together. He too couldn't wait until all of this was over and done with.

"Thanks for letting me come out here and stretch my legs for a second," Sabrina thanked him. "I appreciate it."

"Don't mention it," Mike said. He was a good guy that had gotten caught up in a bad lifestyle. Mike was in it for the money. He never used force or hurt anyone unless he had no other option.

"So what made you get into this type of lifestyle?"

"Money," Mike answered honestly. He was

about to say something else but stopped when two detectives came walking through the parking lot, the beams from their flashlights guiding them where they needed to go. "Come on!" Mike roughly grabbed Sabrina by her arm, rushing her back inside the room.

"What's wrong?" Monica asked. She could tell by how Mike rushed Sabrina inside the room that something wasn't right.

"Two detectives are outside," Mike said, peeking through the blinds. "I think they walking around searching the perimeter."

"Searching the perimeter for what?" Monica asked. Her body language went from relaxed to frantic to scared in a split second.

"I'm sure we about to find out." Mike checked the magazine on his machine gun, slammed the clip, and awaited the detectives' arrival.

twenty

*K*eyon sat in the passenger seat, staring out the window as old school music hummed softly through the speakers. Here he was in the passenger seat of a stolen car, a wing man on a mission he had no knowledge about. Keyon quietly wondered what kind of mess he was about to be walking into.

"What you over there thinking about?" Jesus asked, keeping his eyes on the road. He could tell by how quiet Keyon was that there must have been something on his mind.

"I'm just ready for all this to be over and done with," Keyon said honestly. He feared that when it came time for him and his family to be released, he would either be dead or in jail.

"I just want to let you know that you have been doing a hell of a job," Jesus said. "Trust me, when this is all over, your family is going to love you even more."

"I wouldn't be so sure about that," Keyon chuckled. His relationship with Mya was ruined, and if he didn't figure out a way to get his wife out of this mess, his marriage would be heading down the drain next. "I think you've put me and my family through enough." Keyon turned to face Jesus. "Why don't you do the right thing and just let us all go?"

"I wish I could, but unfortunately I can't right now." Jesus pulled over on a quiet block. "Now listen, I'm going to get in that car and drop it off at this secret location. I need you to get behind the wheel of this car and follow me. Understand?"

"But what's inside the car?" He wanted to know what he was getting into beforehand so he could know how he needed to move.

"Just follow behind me like I said," Jesus snapped as he and Keyon stepped out of the stolen truck. Jesus walked over to the car that Omar said would be waiting for him, removed the keys from off the top of the tire, and got behind the wheel.

Keyon walked around from the passenger side to the driver side and got behind the wheel. Keyon placed the gear in drive, and the first thing that came to his mind was escaping and going to get some help for his family. Keyon had to make a decision, and he had to make it fast. If Keyon went to the cops, he knew all Jesus had to do was make one phone call and his family was as good as dead. So for now he had to continue to do as Jesus had instructed.

Jesus reached over in the glove compartment and removed a piece of paper that held the address to which he was supposed to deliver the car. Jesus placed the car in drive and quickly pulled away from the curb. He had no clue what was inside the car or if it was stolen or what. All he wanted to do was get the car to the destination as soon as possible and be done with it. Jesus wanted to zoom through the streets, but he knew that wouldn't be a wise move, so instead he stuck to the speed limit and followed all traffic laws just to be on the safe side. Any slight slip-up and he could find himself sitting in a jail cell for a very long time.

Jesus stopped at a red light, when he heard a banging sound coming from somewhere in the car. "What the hell is that?" he said out loud. He listened closely again but heard nothing. Taking it as his mind playing tricks on him, Jesus continued to drive. He was only fifteen minutes away from the drop-off location. Jesus peeked through the rearview mirror and saw Keyon keeping a close distance behind him. Jesus admired Keyon's courage and determination to do whatever it took to keep his family alive. If the roles were reversed, Jesus didn't know if he would have been able to do what Keyon was doing at the moment, and for that reason he had to tip his hat to Keyon.

Jesus turned onto a quiet looking street, when he heard the banging sound again.

BANG! BANG! BANG!

Jesus pulled the car over to the side of the road and looked around, when the banging sound erupted again.

BANG! BANG! BANG!

The sound was coming from the trunk. Jesus quickly stepped out of the car and headed toward the back so he could investigate and see what the noise was. Jesus popped the trunk, and inside he saw a woman with her hands and ankles bound together and a frightened look on her face.

"Please help me, please!" the woman begged.

twenty-one

"Hi, I'm detective Tracy." The detective flashed his badge. "Have you heard or seen anything strange tonight?"

"Yes, I heard a loud scream," the witness began. "So I looked out my window and saw a tall man with long dreadlocks throwing a woman into the backseat of a car."

"And what room were you in?" Detective Tracy pulled out his notepad and began scribbling down everything the women was telling him. He had gotten a call about a man tossing a woman in a trunk, and now here he was, standing in the parking lot looking for some answers.

"I'm in room 16," the witness replied.

"If you saw the man with the dreadlocks, would you be able to identify him?"

"I didn't get a great look at him, but I'll try my best," the witness said honestly.

"Thank you, ma'am." Detective Tracy smiled.

"I'm going to go search the perimeter. When I'm done we can go downtown and talk to the sketch artist." Detective Tracy pulled out his flashlight and began his search. In the beginning he didn't have much information, but the longer he stayed on the motel's grounds, the more he was starting to realize that there may have been more to the story. Detective Tracy walked through the parking lot and stopped when he came across a puddle of blood. He quickly called in for backup, kneeled down, and examined the blood. Detective Tracy stood to his feet and walked over to the first door and knocked on it. He wasn't leaving until he screened every last person on the motel grounds, and no one was allowed to leave until his investigation was complete.

twenty-two

*K*eyon sat behind the wheel of the stolen truck and watched as Jesus pulled over, popped the trunk, and stood there. From where Keyon sat it looked like Jesus was talking to someone. "What the hell is going on?" Keyon said to himself as he stepped out of the truck and made his way over to the back of the trunk with Jesus. Keyon walked up and immediately spotted the woman tied up in the trunk. "Who the hell is she, and why the hell is she in the trunk?"

Jesus shrugged. "I don't know, and I don't care." He slammed the trunk shut.

"We can't just leave her in there," Keyon said. "That's not right."

"Listen, she ain't our problem. Our problem is Omar," Jesus reminded him. "And if 'we' don't deliver this car, 'we' going to have a serious problem, and I don't need those types of problems in my life right now!"

"So what we supposed to do? Just leave her in the trunk and deliver her to a group of men and let them just do god knows what to her?" Keyon asked, with his face crumpled up.

"Not my problem."

"That could be someone's mother, sister, or aunt in that trunk," Keyon continued. "This ain't right."

"If I were you I'd be worried about my own wife," Jesus said coldly. "Now get back in the car, follow me, and shut the fuck up." With that said, Jesus got back behind the wheel of the car and pulled away from the curb.

He too felt bad about the woman locked in his trunk. If this was a different circumstance Jesus definitely would have let the woman go free, but unfortunately today he couldn't allow that to happen. He turned the volume up to try to drown out the constant banging on the trunk, but it seemed the louder he turned up the volume, the louder the banging got.

Jesus peeked up at the rearview mirror and saw Keyon still close behind him. A part of him felt kind of bad for Keyon. Jesus knew he had a good heart and wanted to do right, but this wasn't that type of party. The choices were simple: either drop the car off and keep your life, or don't drop the car off and lose your life. This was no-brainer for Jesus. He didn't care who was in the trunk. He was going to drop that car off.

Jesus pulled up in front of a rundown looking warehouse and saw a big fat guy standing out front.

"It's about time you got here," the big man's voice boomed. "We been waiting for this all day." He took the keys from Jesus's hands, with a huge smile on his face.

"Hey, just so you know, it's been a banging sound coming from the trunk," Jesus called out.

"Trust and believe I'mma take care of that," the big man got behind the wheel of the car and pulled it inside the warehouse.

All Jesus could do was shake his head as he walked back over to the stolen truck and stepped in the passenger's seat. "Ight, lets head back to the motel."

Keyon pulled back out into traffic with a sour look on his face. He felt horrible about his participation in helping traffic a human being. Once he and his family were let free Keyon planned on doing some real soul searching and figuring out how he could cleanse his soul once this was all said and done.

"You hungry?" Jesus asked.

"So what you think they going to do with that girl?" Keyon asked, ignoring Jesus's question.

"I don't fucking know, and I don't care!" Jesus snapped. "That's none of our business! We did what we were supposed to do!"

"Did you see the look on that big guy's face?" Keyon shook his head. "I bet there were probably ten other guys in that warehouse."

Jesus shrugged. "Who cares?"

"I care!" Keyon snapped. "What you need to do is start using your 'street cred' to do some good out on the streets instead of using it for destruction."

Jesus pulled his gun from his waistband and jammed it into Keyon's rib cage. "Say another motherfucking word and I'mma have you walking around with a shit bag!"

Keyon peeked up and saw flashing blue lights in his rearview mirror. "Put that gun away. The cops are behind us," he announced.

"Pull this motherfucker over and act normal," Jesus instructed with a no-nonsense look on his face. "You do anything to tip this cop off, and I'm killing you and him!" he threatened.

Keyon pulled the stolen truck over and took a deep breath. His biggest fear was now turning into a reality. He would officially be arrested and placed in jail for a very long time. The first thing that ran through his mind was, what was going to happen to his wife and daughter while he was in jail? Would the gunmen release his family?

Keyon's heart threatened to beat out of his chest as the officer walked up and banged on the driver's window with his flashlight.

twenty-three

"Thank you for your cooperation, ma'am," Detective Tracy said. He then made his way to the next room. He wasn't leaving until he had spoken to and questioned every last guest. So far none of the guests had been any help, but that didn't deter the detective. He just moved on to the next room.

Detective Tracy reached the next room and gave the door a hard, strong knock.

***

"Damn, he's coming to our room next!" Mike peeked out the window at the detective, with a nervous look on his face. "When he knocks on the door I want you to open it, and I'm going to blow his face off," Mike said in a serious tone. He would rather die than go back to jail.

Sabrina stood to her feet. "Hold on, there has to

be a better way to handle this," she said. In the back of her mind Sabrina knew that if Mike killed that detective, she and Mya would more than likely be next, and she couldn't allow that to happen.

"You got a better plan?" Mike asked in a harsh whisper.

"When the detective knocks on the door let me speak to him," Sabrina suggested.

"Do I look stupid to you!?" Mike asked. "The first opportunity you get you'll give us up without even thinking twice about it."

"I do that, then what happens to my daughter?" Sabrina watched his tone. "Trust me, I'll get us out of this."

As soon as the words left her lips, there was a loud knock at the door.

KNOCK! KNOCK! KNOCK!

"Fuck that. I'm about to shoot this cop and get it over with!" Mike grabbed his machine gun, but Monica finally stopped him.

"Use your head for once. Let Sabrina go and talk to the cop!" Monica said as the knocking continued.

KNOCK! KNOCK! KNOCK!

"You say anything to tip that cop off, and your daughter is dead!" Mike grabbed Mya off the bed, and the both of them headed into the bathroom.

"I hope you know what you're doing." Monica sat on the bed and watched as Sabrina walked to the door, took a deep breath, and then opened it. "Good evening, officer, how can I help you?" she asked in a polite tone.

"How you doing, ma'am? The name is Detective Tracy, and I wanted to ask you a couple of questions," he began. "Earlier tonight we believe a woman was abducted right here at this motel."

"Oh my god, are you serious?" Sabrina covered her mouth with her hand for extra emphasis. She knew in order to get the detective to believe her she was going to have to throw it on thick. "That's horrible."

"Did you happen to hear any strange noises or any type of disturbances, ma'am?"

Sabrina shook her head. "No, it's been pretty quiet around here all night."

"Are you here alone?" the detective asked, catching Sabrina off guard.

"Um, no, I'm here with my girlfriend," Sabrina answered quickly.

"Mind if I have a word with her?" the detective asked.

"Sure." Sabrina turned and called over her shoulder, "Baby, come here real quick. There's a detective at the door, and he wants to ask you a few questions."

Monica shoved her gun down into the small of her back as she stood and walked over to the door. "Good evening officer, what seems to be the problem?"

In the bathroom Mya sat on the toilet with a scared look on her face as Mike stood over her with his machine gun aimed directly at her face. Just from the look on his face Mya could tell that if she even made a peep he wouldn't hesitate to shoot her dead right then and there.

"How you doing, ma'am? I was just explaining to your girlfriend that a woman was abducted earlier on tonight, and we were just asking around to see if anyone heard or saw anything."

Monica shook her head. "No, sorry, I didn't hear a thing. Most of the night has been pretty quiet."

"Okay, thank you, ladies, for your cooperation. Enjoy the rest of your night," the detective said, making his way to the next room. Monica closed the door and breathed a sigh of relief.

Sabrina banged on the bathroom door. "Y'all can come out now. The coast is clear!"

Mya rushed out of the bathroom and hugged her mother tightly. "Mommy, I'm ready to go home."

"Don't worry, baby, we'll be home soon," Sabrina promised, gently rubbing Mya's back. "Your father is out doing what he gotta do so we can go home."

twenty-four

*K*eyon rolled the driver's window down and placed a fake smile on his face. "How you doing, officer? What seems to be the problem?"

"You didn't see that stop sign back there? You ran right through it."

"Sorry about that, officer. I didn't even realize I ran the stop sign. I can assure you something like that will never happen again," Keyon said in a friendly tone.

"License and registration, please!" the officer said in a firm tone as he shined his light all throughout the inside of the vehicle.

"Here you go, officer." Keyon handed the officer all the info he had requested. The officer took the license and registration and headed back to his car.

"Soon as he come back I'm blowing his head off!" Jesus said, sitting his gun on his lap. He could tell by how hostile the officer was acting that this wasn't going to end prettily.

"Hold on, I think can maybe talk my way out of this," Keyon said as his mind began trying to come up with a plan on how to get him and Jesus out of this situation without anyone getting hurt.

"Well you better think of something quick, because if that cop even blinks the wrong way it's on and popping," Jesus said in a matter-of-fact tone.

Keyon kept his eyes on the side mirror, making sure to keep an eye on the officer at all times. Keyon knew that the truck was stolen, so he was trying to formulate a good excuse that could get them off the hook, but at the moment his mind was drawing a blank.

"Fuck that. I say we pull off right now and take our chances," Jesus suggested. Keyon could immediately tell that Jesus was starting to get antsy, and in a situation like this everyone needed to remain calm.

"Here he come. Act normal," Keyon said, giving Jesus the heads up.

The officer walked back to the driver's side window and leaned down. "This car has been

WRONG PLACE WRONG TIME

reported stolen. Step out of the car, please."

"There has to be some type of mistake," Keyon said with the friendly smile still on his face. "This is my cousin's car. I can call her right now if you'd like."

"Step out of the car, please!" The officer placed his hand on the handle of his gun.

"Officer, this is all just a big misunderstanding. I told you this belongs to . . ." Keyon's sentence was cut short when the officer roughly opened his door and snatched him out of the driver's seat and forcefully slammed him against the car.

"You got any drugs or weapons on you?" the officer asked as he began to search Keyon. The officer pulled out a pair of handcuffs, but just as he was about to put them on Keyon's wrist, the officer's head exploded like a melon.

Keyon spun around and saw the officer's body lying face-first on the ground, with a gaping hole in the back of his head.

"Come on, we gotta go!" Jesus yelled, snapping Keyon out of his trance. The two men quickly ran and jumped back inside the stolen getaway truck. This time Jesus was behind the wheel.

"You killed him," Keyon said still in a bit of shock. "Do you realize what you just done?

"It was either him or us!" Jesus yelled. "And I ain't going back to jail!"

"Do you realize what you just did?" Keyon's mind was racing a hundred miles per second. "When they catch us they going to throw us under the jail!"

"We ain't going to get caught! Now shut the fuck up because you making me nervous!" Jesus yelled as he saw two more cop cars zoom past him headed in the opposite direction. Jesus made a right and then a quick left before stopping the car in the middle of the street.

"What are you doing?" Keyon asked, looking at Jesus like he was crazy.

"We can't stay in this car a second longer!" Jesus and Keyon jumped out of the truck and took off on foot. Keyon was scared to death. He was no longer worried about going to jail, but now his main was to try to stay alive.

"Damn!" Keyon huffed, out of breath. He was out of shape and couldn't remember the last time he had run this fast or for such a long period of time. "I'm done. I can't run no more!" Keyon bent over placing both hands on his knees as he tried to suck up as much air as possible. His chest was on fire, and his lungs felt as if he had just drunk a whole glass of acid.

"Come on, we can't stop. We have to keep going!" Jesus grabbed Keyon, forcing him to continue to keep his feet moving. Jesus would rather kill Keyon than get caught by the cops, because he knew the chances of Keyon spilling the beans were very high. As the two men ran down the street, Jesus noticed an older man step out of his vehicle and head toward the front door of his house. Jesus quickly hopped the fence and grabbed the old man by the back collar of his shirt, then violently flung him down to the ground.

"Please don't hurt me . . . please," the old man begged for his life.

"Give me the car keys, old man, and we'll be on

our way," Jesus told the old man. He didn't want to have to kill the old man, but he wouldn't hesitate if the old man didn't meet all of his demands. The old man quickly stood to his feet, removed the car keys from his pocket, and held them out. Jesus quickly snatched the keys from the old man's hand and then turned and stole on him, knocking the old man out with one punch.

Jesus and Keyon quickly jumped into the new car and drove off like a couple of maniacs

twenty-five

*M*eanwhile, back inside the motel room, everyone was sleep, that is, everyone except for Mike. He sat on the floor with his back pressed against the wall and his feet crossed at the ankles. Mike did his best to try to not think negatively about this entire situation, but that was easier said than done. Once again Jesus had been out of the motel room longer than anticipated. With everything that been going on Mike found himself becoming a bit more paranoid. He too was tired of being cooped up in the motel room all day, and he found himself getting restless. Mike was tired of babysitting and was ready to move on to the next job.

***

An hour later Mike felt himself getting ready to doze off, when the front door opened and in walked Jesus and Keyon.

"How did everything go?" Mike asked.

"Smooth like butter," Jesus lied, helping himself to a seat on the floor. He was worn out and needed to rest. "Get you some rest. We got a big job coming up soon."

"What big job?" Mike asked curiously.

"I'll tell you about it in the morning," Jesus said with a smile as he leaned his head back against the wall and shut his eyes. "Get you some rest."

Keyon walked straight to the bed, lay down, and held his wife in his arms.

"You okay, baby?" Sabrina snuggled into her husband's chest. She was just happy to have her husband back in one piece. "I was worried about you."

"I'm fine, baby. Get you some rest," Keyon said, gently massaging Sabrina's scalp with his fingers. He knew his wife was scared, which meant he had to be strong. "This will all be over in no time, baby. Don't you even worry about it," he whispered with his eyes closed. Within minutes both Keyon and Sabrina were sound asleep.

***

The next morning Keyon woke up and noticed that Jesus was already awake, and from the looks of it he was in deep thought. "Good morning, what you doing up so early?"

"Haven't you ever heard the early bird gets the worm?" Jesus chuckled. "If I were you I would take advantage of this time that you have to sleep, because in the next few hours we will be doing a job that'll more than likely change your life forever. Matter of fact, it's going to change all of our lives."

"What's the big job?" Keyon asked.

"Just know if we can pull this job off, you and your family are free to go," Jesus promised.

Jesus's words put a big smile on Keyon's face. There was nothing more he wanted than his freedom. At this point in time he and his family deserved it. He just hoped and prayed he was still alive once the job was over.

"You ready to go back to your normal life?" Jesus asked.

"Is that a trick question?"

Jesus smiled. "It's almost over, kid. I know I didn't come all this way just to come all this way. The finish line is right around the corner." Jesus quickly grabbed his gun when out of the corner of his eye he saw the front door open and a figure dressed in all black step inside.

"Hold your fire. It's just me," Monica said with two big bags of McDonald's in her hand. "Damn, I go get breakfast and you ready to kill me," she joked as she distributed all of the food to everyone.

Mike took a bite out of his breakfast biscuit and then got straight to the point. "Okay, so what's this top-secret job you got for us?"

Jesus smiled. "Well just know that if we can pull this job off, we'll have enough money to pay Omar back and get back to our regular lives." Jesus nodded at Keyon. "That goes for you and your family as well."

"So what's the job?" Mike asked again. He was tired of playing this silly game of cat and mouse.

"We taking down a bank," Jesus announced. He

had been thinking long and hard about this. Jesus had been planning the bank heist for the past month. He had done all the research, and he knew which employees worked what day, what time the security guards went on break, the whole nine. The problem wasn't robbing the bank—that was the easy part. The difficult part would be getting away with the money, especially since the nearest highway was two miles away from the bank. That's why Jesus had never moved forward with the bank robbery, but now he felt as if his back was up against the wall. Jesus knew this was the quickest way they would be able to get Omar his money and get him out of their lives once and for all.

"Jesus, do you hear what you're saying?" Mike asked just to make sure. "We ain't never did a job this big before." Mike was afraid that maybe Jesus was trying to take things too far. Robbing houses and drug dealers was one thing, but robbing a bank was an entirely different ball game. That was something that people only did on TV. "It's too risky."

"We always going to be last on the food chain if

we don't take any risk," Jesus pointed out. His main objective was to get enough money to pay Omar back. He was tired of being under the man's thumb and having to do whatever he said when he said it. "I'm tired of working for Omar!" he said. "We are all our own bosses, but until we pay Omar back we have to do whatever he says, and I'm not cool with that."

"I agree," Monica added her two cents. "I say let's do it, because I'm afraid the longer we are in debt to Omar, the better our chances of dying are." She figured, what did they really have to lose?

"I don't know about this one," Mike said. He was still on the fence and not too sure about this whole robbing a bank thing. Too many things could go wrong in a bank, there were too many unknowns, and that's what really had Mike nervous. Not to mention the chances of them getting caught were much higher.

"We don't have too much of a choice," Jesus said, turning his attention to Keyon. "How you feel about this, Keyon?"

"Count me in." Keyon's response surprised everyone. Everyone was expecting him to say the opposite, but just like Jesus he too was just ready for this whole nightmare to be over and done with.

"Baby, are you crazy?" Sabrina sat up on the bed. "You can't rob a bank. You're going to get yourself killed."

Keyon stood to his feet and looked Jesus in his eyes. "I do this one last job, and me and my family are free to go?"

Jesus nodded. "Absolutely."

"Can I get your word on that?" Keyon extended his hand.

"You got my word," Jesus replied as the two men shook on it.

"Baby, I think you're making a big mistake," Sabrina said with a concerned look on her face. The last thing she wanted was for her husband to end up dead or in jail, and she just couldn't see anything good coming from robbing a bank.

"What other options do I have?" Keyon asked. In his mind it was either do this or continue to be slaves to the stick-up crew, and to him this was a no-brainer. "I don't know about you, but I'm ready to go home."

"I want to go home too, baby, but I don't want to go home alone." Sabrina grabbed Keyon's hand. "You're all I got, and I can't afford to lose you."

"You not going to lose me, baby." Keyon looked Sabrina in her eyes. "Trust me."

Jesus then turned his focus to Mike. "We just waiting on you."

"Ight, fuck it, I'm in," Mike said reluctantly. He didn't really want to go along with it, but it was three against one. "The majority rules."

twenty-six

*T*he three men sat in a restaurant enjoying a meal just in case it turned out to be their last. Each man sat at the table with a nervous look on his face. They were focused but still nervous.

"After today we will all be free," Jesus said, trying to lighten the mood. He could feel the nervous energy in the air and was trying to get rid of it. "This job is going to be a piece of cake. Keyon all I need you to do is stay in the getaway car and keep the engine running. Me and Mike will take care of everything else."

"How long will y'all be inside the bank?" Keyon asked, shoveling a fork full of eggs into his mouth.

"Four minutes tops," Jesus answered quickly. "This is going to be a smooth operation."

Once the men finished eating they exited the restaurant and piled into the stolen car that awaited them. Keyon pulled away from the curb, and at that point he knew there was no turning back. Whatever was going to happen was just going to happen. It was all in God's hands now. Keyon glanced up at the rearview mirror and saw Jesus and Mike loading their weapons with serious looks on their faces.

"Four minutes," Keyon kept repeating over and over again in his head. Four minutes didn't sound like a lot, but when the stakes were this high four minutes could feel like a lifetime.

Keyon pulled up across the street from the bank, placed the gear in park, and took a deep breath. There was no turning back now. "Okay, four minutes in and out!"

"If you see any cops, beep the horn repeatedly!" Mike said as he pulled his ski mask down over his face.

"Come on, let's do this!" Jesus said as he and Mike stepped out of the stolen car and headed straight for the bank.

Keyon sat behind the wheel with a nervous look on his face. He watched Jesus and Mike walk, until they disappeared inside the bank. Keyon looked down at his hand and noticed it was shaking uncontrollably. He couldn't see inside the bank, but he could only imagine what was going on inside. All he could do was hope and pray that things went well on the inside.

***

"So this is it," Monica said with a smile. "After today you go back to being a free woman again."

Sabrina smiled. "And I can't wait. The first thing I'm going to do is take a hot bubble bath and drink a glass of wine."

"That don't sound too bad. I may have to do the same," Monica laughed. She was happy that she and Sabrina had found a way to get on good terms, especially after such a bumpy start.

"You know, you're not too bad after all," Sabrina said. "Maybe when this is all over with we can go out and get some drinks or something."

"I think I may just take you up on that offer." Monica smiled as she glanced down at her watch.

"The men should be inside the bank by now, so this long nightmare will be over in the next few minutes."

twenty-seven

"Everybody down on the floor now!" Jesus yelled as he stepped inside the bank and made his way straight toward the security guard that stood on post. He aimed his machine gun down toward the guard's legs and pulled the trigger.

"Argh!" the guard howled in pain. He could feel the bone in his leg snap from the impact of the bullet. Everyone else inside the bank watched in horror as they collapsed down to the floor. Jesus quickly reached down and removed the gun from the guard's holster.

"Nobody fucking move!" Jesus yelled as he watched Mike hop over the counter and begin collecting money.

"Open this drawer right now before I blow your head off!" Mike warned as the older woman did as she was told. Once the drawer was open, Mike shoved the woman down onto the floor and began stuffing money into his duffle bag. Once that drawer was empty, he moved on to the next drawer. "Get yo' ass up!" Mike growled as he grabbed a scrawny looking man by the collar of his shirt and forced him to open up the next drawer. Once the drawer was open Mike hit the man over the top of the head with his gun, causing a huge gash to open on the man's head. Mike quickly emptied all the money from the drawer down into the duffle bag. Once the duffle bag was full he tossed it over the counter to Jesus. Mike then grabbed the second duffle bag that hung around his neck. He walked behind the counter and a door. As he reached for the doorknob, he saw that it was locked. He quickly turned to the next closest employee and snatched her up to her feet by her hair. "Open this motherfucking door!"

"I don't have the key," the woman said in a frantic tone as tears rolled down her face. Without warning Mike back slapped the woman down to the floor. "I'm not going to ask you again!"

While all this was going on a brave employee lay facedown on the floor watching his fellow coworker take a beating. The brave man took a deep breath, hopped up off the floor, ran toward the counter, and hit the alarm.

Mike's head snapped in the direction of the brave employee when he heard the alarm going off. He walked straight up to the employee and shot him five times at point-blank range.

***

Keyon sat outside in the getaway car with a nervous look on his face. He damn near pissed in his pants when he heard the alarm sound. He had no clue on what was going on inside the bank, but whatever it was it couldn't have been good. Thoughts of driving off and leaving Jesus and Mike for dead crossed his mind. The longer Keyon sat there, the more he wanted just to drive off and secure his freedom. In the distance Keyon thought he heard what sounded like a police siren.

***

Back inside the bank, Mike filled up the second duffle bag with as much money as he could before hopping back over the counter. Mike and Jesus then quickly made a beeline for the front door and exited the bank.

Keyon looked over to his left and saw Jesus and Mike running out of the bank. He quickly threw the car into gear and drove. Once both men were back in the car, Keyon mashed down on the gas pedal, causing the car to leap into action.

"Come on, come on, let's go!" Jesus yelled. "We did that shit!" he yelled with his voice full of excitement. Jesus and Mike began celebrating in the car, when Keyon stomped down on the brakes causing everyone's body to jerk forward.

A cop car came to a skidding stop, blocking the getaway car.

"Shit!" Keyon cursed as he threw the gear in reverse and mashed down on the gas. Keyon had one hand on the steering wheel and one hand on the back of the passenger seat headrest as he drove backward at a fast speed.

"Fuck this!" Jesus spat as he rolled down the passenger window and hung half way out and opened fire on the two cop cars in front of him. Mike watched from the backseat as the machine gun bullets decorated the cop cars with bullet holes, causing them to stop their pursuit.

Keyon stomped down on the brakes and cut the wheel hard all the way to the left while switching the gear from reverse back to drive all at the same time. Mike hung on for dear life as the car did a complete 360 and kept on moving, never missing a beat.

"Yeeeeeah!" Mike yelled, cheering Keyon on from the backseat. He couldn't believe how Keyon was able to handle the car the way he did. Mike had never seen anything like that in his life.

Keyon smiled as he cut the wheel hard to the left, guiding the stolen car down a one-way street. This was the first time he had felt accepted by the guys.

"You did that shit!" Jesus smiled as he ruffled Keyon's hair. Keyon smiled proudly as he avoided getting on the highway. He figured they could buy more time by staying on all of the back roads

twenty-eight

Sabrina paced back and forth with a nervous look on her face. It had been hours since the men left, and no one had a clue what was going on. No phone calls, no text messages, no nothing.

"Please sit down. You're starting to make me nervous," Monica said. She too was beginning to wonder if everything was alright with the men, but the more Sabrina continued to pace the floor, the more nervous it made Monica. "Relax."

"How can I relax?" Sabrina asked, looking at Monica like she was crazy. "They said this job would only take four minutes, and they've been gone for hours now!"

"Well you pacing back and forth is not going to make them get here any faster," Monica pointed out as she turned on the TV to the news. "Look, if they'd been caught or captured it would have been all over the news by now," she said, in an attempt to comfort Sabrina. "So you see, you're worrying about nothing."

"It may be nothing to you, but my husband is everything to me!" Sabrina countered as she flopped down on the bed and cried her eyes out. She didn't like the fact that everyone was so nonchalant about everything.

"It's going to be okay, Mommy." Mya came over and tried to comfort her mother. Mya didn't really care for her father, but she still felt bad for her mother and hated to see her suffering like this. "Just know, in the worst-case scenario we always got each other."

"Thanks, baby." Sabrina hugged Mya tightly.

***

"We got company!" Keyon announced, looking through the rearview mirror as two cop cars trailed their car. "We have to split up on foot!"

"Hell no!" Jesus huffed, looking out the back window.

"Wait, Keyon may be right!" Mike said. "We need to split up and bail on foot before the eye in the sky gets a beam on us." He knew it wouldn't be long before the helicopter was on their trail, and once they were on the helicopter's radar they were as good as done.

"Okay, we going to split up. If anyone gets caught keep your mouth shut, and I'll make sure your family gets your share." Jesus extended his fist. "I'll meet y'all back at the room. Be safe!"

"Be safe!" Keyon and Mike said as they all bumped fist with one another. Keyon bent the curve at a high speed and stomped down on the brakes. When the car came to a complete stop each man hopped out and ran in their own direction. Keyon made it about twenty yards away before several cop cars surrounded the getaway car. Keyon hopped a short fence and disappeared into the woods.

Jesus ran down a hill, looked over his shoulder, and noticed a cop and a detective not too far behind him. Without thinking twice Jesus aimed his machine gun over his shoulder sending several reckless shots in the cops' direction. The shots caused the cops to hit the deck in an attempt to avoid getting a bullet lodged in their body.

Jesus wasn't playing around with the police. With all the innocent black men the cops had been killing lately for no reason, he knew if they caught him he was as good as dead. Jesus cut down a quiet street running full speed. He glanced over his shoulder and saw a detective still hot on his trail. "Shit!" Jesus cursed. He knew in order to get this detective off his trail he was going to have to kill him. As Jesus ran he saw a woman taking her groceries inside her house. Jesus quickly jumped the fence, ran through the woman's yard, and then pushed his way into her home. The woman screamed loudly as she dramatically fell down to the floor. Jesus scrambled through the house, knocking things over as he ran, in an attempt to slow down the detective behind him. Jesus exploded through the back and ran through the backyard.

Detective Tracy entered the house, maneuvered around all the obstacles that were lying out in front of him, and ran out the back door. He watched as the masked man hopped the tall fence that led to the house next door. Detective Tracy ran and hopped the fence. There was no way he was letting the masked man get away. If Tracy was able to get a clean shot on the gunman, he wouldn't hesitate to take it.

Jesus ran across a busy street, barely avoiding getting hit by several cars. Multiple drivers cursed and beeped their horns out of frustration. Jesus ran full speed through someone else's yard and then cut around to the back of the house.

Detective Tracy ran across the street, ran through the yard, and around the house. When he reached the back of the house the masked man was nowhere in sight. Detective Tracy quickly pulled his gun from his holster. He knew the masked man couldn't have gotten far in that short period of time. The detective slowly crept through the back yard taking cautious steps, when he heard what sounded like leaves crunching under someone's foot. Detective Tracy spun around, and then everything went black.

When the detective turned around, Jesus hit him in the temple with his machine gun, knocking the detective unconscious. Jesus thought about shooting the detective in his face, but knew that would draw too much attention, so instead he just jogged through the back yard, hopped the fence, and disappeared around the corner.

twenty-nine

K eyon jogged out of the woods, looked around, and noticed the police had checkpoints on certain streets. "Damn!" he cursed as he saw cops searching cars looking for the armed and dangerous bank robbers. Keyon thought about taking off his ski mask to try to see if he wouldn't be noticed by the cops, but quickly decided against it. Instead Keyon jogged to his left, where there weren't too many cops. Even if he didn't get caught right now, there was no way for him to make it past the checkpoints, but for now Keyon had to think fast. He slowly jogged down a street lined with nice houses on both sides. Keyon saw a car pulling into the garage on one of the houses, and he quickly snuck under the door before it shut.

A beautiful caramel-skinned woman stepped out of the car, with a small bag in her hand. She turned around, and when she looked up she almost had a heart attack. "Oh my god, please don't hurt me," she begged, with her hands raised in surrender.

"As long as you do as I say won't nobody get hurt," Keyon said with his gun aimed at the woman's chest. He grabbed the woman by her arm and escorted her to the front door. The woman fumbled with her keys for a second before finally opening the door. "What do you want from me?"

"Have a seat!" Keyon ordered as he opened the woman's refrigerator and removed an apple. He ate the apple like an animal and then helped himself to another one. "Is there anyone else in the house?"

The woman shook her head. "No, it's just me."

"You live here by yourself?"

The woman nodded. "Yes."

"Are you expecting anyone to come over tonight? A boyfriend? Fiance or anything?" Keyon asked as he began to look around. The woman had a nice house and seemed to be doing well for herself.

"Me and my boyfriend broke up two weeks ago," the woman answered.

Keyon took one look at the woman and couldn't understand how a man could let such a beautiful woman get away. "Why did y'all break up?"

"He was cheating with a girl he said was like his sister." The woman used air quotes with her fingers when she said sister.

"What's your name?"

"Melissa," the woman answered.

"Well, Melissa, this is how this is going to work," Keyon began. "I'm going to stay here until this heat dies down, which will probably be tomorrow night at the latest. You're going to relax and not do anything stupid. Then tomorrow I will leave and you can go on with your regular life," Keyon explained. "You okay with that?"

Melissa nodded her head. She was afraid, but for some reason she felt safe with the masked man. There was a certain calmness about him. "Thank you."

"For what?" Keyon asked, with a confused look on his face.

"For not hurting me or trying to rape me," Melissa said as she kicked her shoes off.

"You don't have to thank me for that," Keyon

said as he grabbed Melissa's pocket book from off the table and began to fish through it. He removed her cell phone. "Sorry, but I have to hold on to this until I leave."

Melissa waved him off. "Hold it for as long as you want. Don't nobody call me," she chuckled. "So you were one of the guys who robbed that bank?"

Keyon nodded. He felt bad about his actions but had no choice but to move forward with them.

"It was all over the radio," Melissa said. "They said a few people got shot, but you don't strike me as the violent type."

"I didn't shoot those people," Keyon said quickly. He was surprised by how fast the word had spread. "Can you turn on the news, please?"

"Sure."

As soon as the TV came on Keyon saw a reporter with a microphone held up to her mouth standing in front of the bank, with several cops and yellow caution tape in the background. Immediately Keyon thought about Sabrina. He knew if she was watching the news she was probably losing her mind by now.

He could only imagine what was going on in her mind at the moment. Keyon knew if the roles were reversed he would have been thinking the worst and probably counting her out as well. He wished there was a way he could somehow get in touch with his wife just to let her know that he was okay, but Jesus had taken all of their phones.

"Can you breathe okay with that mask on?" Melissa asked from the couch.

"It's a little hot, but hey"—Keyon shrugged—"sometimes you gotta do what you gotta do," he said, helping himself to a seat on the other couch that sat in the living room.

"So what now?" Melissa asked.

"Now we wait."

thirty

*M*ike woke up in the middle of the night lying on a large pile of leaves. He called himself hiding in the woods, but as Mike hid, the police set up shop at each exit, causing him to be stuck in the woods for the entire night. Mike slowly made it to his feet and looked around, checking his surroundings. From where he stood the coast seemed to be clear. Mike walked through the woods looking for an exit. He couldn't wait to make it back to the room and tell everyone about the crazy night he had. Mike knew they were all probably worried sick about him, and he couldn't wait to see their faces when he walked through that door. Mike's wonderful thoughts came to an end when he heard footsteps crunching through the woods. Before Mike got a chance to turn around to see who the footsteps belonged to, he froze when he heard someone yell, "Freeze!"

Once Mike heard the voice behind him yell

freeze, he immediately knew the man was a cop. He thought about turning around and having a shootout with the cop, but Mike knew he would have gotten shot down before he could even turn around.

"Get down on the ground now!" the officer yelled.

With no other options Mike took off in a sprint as the sound of the officer opening fire on him sounded off loudly.

Mike ran recklessly through the woods, when he felt a bullet explode in the back of his thigh, sending him crashing face-first down to the dirt. Not the type to give up, Mike began army crawling on his stomach. He was willing to fight until he took his last breath. All that was going through Mike's mind at the moment was spending the rest of his life in prison.

"Don't move!" the officer yelled, with his gun trained on Mike.

"Fuck you!" Mike snarled as he reached for his gun that rested on his hip.

"Don't do it!" the officer warned.

Mike continued to reach for his weapon. He would rather die than spend the rest of his life in jail. Mike's hand touched the handle of his gun, when the officer shot him dead right where he stood. The officer slowly walked over to Mike's body, removed the gun from his waistband, and then kneeled down to check to see if he could find a pulse. "Damn," the officer said in a harsh whisper as he grabbed his walkie-talkie and called it in.

thirty-one

*M*onica stood peeking through the blinds. It had been hours now and still no word from anyone. On every station on TV a reporter was reporting about the bank robbery that had taken place. The longer she looked out the window, the more Monica hoped something good might happen.

"Can you please get out of the window? You're making me even more nervous," Sabrina said. She had been watching Monica stand in the window for the last three hours, which meant she had no clue if the men were dead or alive. "Relax!"

"How can I relax? It's been almost twenty-four hours since the men left!" Monica pointed out.

"What happened to 'calm down and everything is going to be alright'?"

"All that shit went out the window!" Monica said. "Every news station is reporting the bank robbery, every cop in the city is probably hunting them down as we speak!" The thing that really bothered Monica was not knowing. The less she knew about what was going on, the more her mind began to wander and think the craziest things. Monica's mind was definitely playing tricks on her.

"Well what's plan B?" Sabrina asked. She was tired of sitting in the room. If the men were in trouble, the first thing they should have done was vacated that room. Why sit around and wait for trouble to come to you?

"I don't have one!" Monica yelled out of frustration. She was trying to think of a plan, but with so many things running through her mind, it made it damn near impossible to think about anything.

"Well I say we stay here for another hour to see if the men show up. If they don't I say we go back to my place. At least there we can think freely and don't have to worry about anyone coming to capture us," Sabrina suggested. She knew once she and Mya were out of the room they had a better chance at trying to escape. Sabrina was ready to get this nightmare over with, even if it meant risking her own life. She was tired of just sitting around like a lump on a log. If she wanted her freedom she was going to have to fight for it, and she was willing to fight to the death if she had to.

"Do you guys live in a nice neighborhood?" Monica asked. The idea about them leaving the motel room didn't seem like a bad one at the moment. Just as Monica got ready to say something else, the front door opened and in walked Jesus with a duffle bag hung over his shoulder. "Oh my god!" Monica ran and hugged him tighter than she had ever hugged him before. "I thought you were dead!"

"You know I ain't letting no punk-ass cops kill me," Jesus said in a smooth tone. The truth was he was afraid, and happy to have made it back to the motel safe and in one piece. Jesus looked straight ahead and saw Sabrina standing in the middle of the floor, with tears running down her face. It was at that moment he knew Keyon was probably dead or in jail.

"Where's my husband?" Sabrina asked. The tears were now pouring down. "Is he dead? Please don't tell me he's dead."

"We got into a little jam," Jesus began. "We all

had to split up, so I have no idea if Keyon is dead or alive," Jesus said honestly. At the moment all Jesus was worried about was saving himself.

"So you just left him for dead?" Sabrina asked. "You use my husband to help you make money, and then when the heat comes down you just leave him for dead?"

"Listen, I didn't leave anyone for dead; we all split up! We had to, the cops were on all of our asses," Jesus tried to explain. "But before we split I had a conversation with Keyon, and I told him if anything happened to him that I would take care of his family financially." Jesus reached down into the duffle bag and handed Sabrina three large stacks of cash.

Sabrina looked down at the money in her hand and then back up at Jesus. "No amount of money can replace my husband."

"Look, either you can take this money and go home, or you can go home with no money and no husband. The choice is yours!" Jesus spat. He was doing the best he could to keep his word, but Sabrina was trying to make it difficult for him.

Without warning, Sabrina spun and slapped Jesus across his face. "Fuck you and your money!" she yelled, and then disrespectfully tossed the bills up in Jesus's face. Sabrina then melted down to the floor and cried her eyes out.

Mya sat on the bed listening to the entire exchange. She slowly slid off the bed and got on the floor to try to comfort her mother. "It's going to be okay, Mommy," she whispered while rubbing Sabrina's back. Within a three-day span, both women had lost their lovers. "We still have each other."

Sabrina cried like her life was over. She had lost her best friend, her lover, as well as her business partner. Now for the rest of her life she would have to live with a hole in her heart.

"I'm sorry," Monica said with a hurt look on her face. It hurt her heart to see Sabrina on the floor crying like that. She just wished there was something she could do to comfort her.

"Y'all free to go!" Jesus announced. He too had

a sad look on his face as he bent down to pick up all the money that was scattered all around the floor. If there was something he could have done differently, he would have. Jesus never wanted or expected this to happen, but sometimes that's just how the game goes.

"I'm not going anywhere!" Sabrina sobbed. "I'm not giving up on my husband. I'm staying one more day to see if he shows up," she announced.

thirty-two

*K*eyon woke up from a deep sleep. He was so tired that he didn't even remember falling asleep. Keyon yawned, stretched, and then looked around and noticed that Melissa was nowhere in sight. "Shit!" he cursed as he hopped to his feet and searched the entire house. Empty.

"Fuck!" Keyon yelled as he melted down to the floor. He just knew that any second the front door would be kicked open, followed by several cops in riot gear coming to lock him up. Deep down inside Keyon couldn't blame Melissa for escaping when the opportunity presented itself, because he would have done the same thing if the roles were reversed.

Keyon sat on the floor as thoughts of his wife and daughter flashed through his mind. He could only imagine the amount of stress he was putting on them. The sound of the front door opening snapped Keyon out of his thoughts. He quickly hopped to his feet with his gun aimed and ready to fire.

Melissa turned the corner alone with a bag of food in her hand. "Whoa! Relax."

"Where the hell have you been?" Keyon growled.

"You were asleep, so I went out to get us some breakfast," Melissa said, as if what she did was no big deal. "You looked so peaceful, I didn't want to disturb you."

Keyon lowered his weapon for the moment. He wasn't sure if the woman was trying to rock him to sleep or if she was just genuinely a nice person.

"I hope you like bacon, eggs, and pancakes," Melissa said, placing the food on the table.

"Thank you," Keyon said as he sat down and had breakfast with the stranger.

"Well I have good news for you," Melissa said, placing a piece of bacon in her mouth. "When I went out to go get the food I noticed that the coast was clear," she said. "All the checkpoints and cops are all gone."

"All of them?" Keyon asked with a raised brow. He still wasn't too sure if he was able to trust the woman that sat across from him.

Melissa nodded her head. "Yup, but now I'm sad because that means you're going to be leaving soon." The truth was Melissa was enjoying the company. It was nice to have someone to talk to.

Keyon swallowed his food whole and then stood to his feet. "I'm sorry for just barging into your home like this. Thank you for your hospitality and not going to the cops," he said, extending his hand.

"No, thank you for being a gentleman." Melissa smiled. "I can tell you're a good person. Please stop robbing banks," she said as the two enjoyed a quick laugh. Melissa shook Keyon's hand. "You take care of yourself."

"You do the same," Keyon said as he finally removed the ski mask from his face and made his exit.

"Need a ride?" Melissa asked.

"No, you've already done enough," Keyon protested. "I couldn't possibly ask you for anything else."

"You didn't ask me, I'm offering. There's a difference." Melissa smiled.

"No thank you." Keyon turned and made his exit. He left the property counting his blessings. He was happy to be alive as well as free. Keyon walked about five blocks until he spotted a bus stop. Keyon helped himself to a seat and awaited the bus's arrival. The motel was on the other side of town, so Keyon knew it would take him a while to make it back to the motel. In his mind he could see the look on Sabrina's and Mya's faces when he walked through the door, and he couldn't wait to turn that into a reality.

thirty-three

Jesus sat at the table in the motel room counting
out all the money he had gotten away with from
the bank robbery. He had enough money to finally
pay Omar off and get out of debt once and for all. But
what was more important was after Jesus paid Omar
back his money he still had a small fortune left over.

"How we looking over there?" Monica asked as
she packed away all of their things.

"We looking real good," Jesus replied. Today he
was in a good mood. To be able to get out of bed with
Omar was a blessing. Jesus knew if he didn't come
up with that money a small war was likely to occur.
Jesus looked over at Sabrina, and immediately he felt
bad for her. She had refused to leave the motel room
until her husband returned. The news had announced
that one of the gunmen had been killed, but they
refused to reveal a name as of yet. "Hey, you okay
over there?"

Sabrina nodded. "I'm okay," she said in a tone

just above a whisper. Her spirits were low, and she badly needed something to snap her out of the funk she was in.

The entire room froze when they heard a knock at the door. Everyone looked at one another before Jesus stood from the table with a gun in his hand and headed to the door. He looked through the peephole and opened the door. Everyone held their breath as Keyon walked through the front door.

Sabrina hopped off the bed and ran and jumped on top of Keyon, tackling him down to the floor, where she planted kisses all over his face. "Oh my god, I thought you were dead!" she cried.

Jesus and Monica looked on with smiles on their faces. Keyon walking through the front door really lit up the entire room and filled it with energy.

Keyon stood to his feet, and Mya walked over and hugged her father. The three of them enjoyed a much-needed nice long family hug.

Keyon showing up meant that Mike was the one who had been killed. Jesus never wanted to lose a man on the job, but it came with the game.

"Give me a second, baby, I need to have a word with Jesus real quick," Keyon said, facing Jesus for the first time.

"I have to go pay Omar his money. Why don't you take that ride with me so we can talk?" Jesus suggested.

Keyon turned and looked at Sabrina. "Get all of our stuff ready. When I come back, we out of here."

"Okay, baby." Sabrina smiled brightly. She was elated to have her husband back safe and sound. Now finally they could go back to their normal lives.

***

Jesus pulled away from the curb with a smile on his face. The sun was shining bright, he had a boatload of cash, and to top it off Keyon had made it back in one piece. "I'm glad you made it back in one piece," Jesus said, keeping his eyes glued to the road. "We were all starting to get worried about you."

"Yesterday was the scariest day of my life," Keyon admitted. "I didn't know if I was going to live, die, or end up in someone's prison."

"I know you heard by now that Mike didn't make it," Jesus said, and immediately Keyon could hear the hurt in his voice.

"Damn, I'm sorry to hear that." Keyon paused for a second. "I want to thank you for keeping your word and letting me and my family go."

"If a man doesn't have his word, that man is not really a man," Jesus countered. "You dug down deep and did what you had to do for your family, and that's all that matters."

"I can't even lie. Going on all these missions with you guys did add a little bit of adventure to my life." Keyon smiled. "But I don't see how y'all can do this for a living."

"I did a lot of thinking last night, and yesterday was my last job. I'm officially retired," Jesus announced. He hadn't even broken the news to Monica. Keyon was the first person he was revealing this to.

"It takes a big man to walk away from all this, and I respect you for that." Keyon gave Jesus his props.

Jesus pulled up and saw Omar's truck already sitting waiting for him. "I'll be right back." Jesus exited the car and slid into the backseat of the truck.

"It's all there." Jesus handed Omar a small bag full of cash.

Omar peeked inside the bag and smiled. "You got the perfect name because you damn sure pulled off a miracle."

A smirk danced on Jesus's lips. "That's what rock stars do."

"So tell me, what's next for you?" Omar asked. He admired Jesus's drive and courage.

"I don't know. I think me and Monica will probably go on vacation somewhere and enjoy some of this money," Jesus said.

"You know you're still in debt to me, right?" Omar said, throwing it out there.

"Bullshit!" Jesus snapped. "Everything I owe you is in that bag, plus some!"

"Did you kill the family yet?" Omar asked.

"Omar, I told you that's not necessary," Jesus

said. "If it wasn't for Keyon, I wouldn't have been able to pull off that last job."

"Not my problem," Omar said with a straight face. He could care less about Keyon or his family. It was his job to tie all loose ends, and that's just what he planned on doing.

"Omar, please don't do this. Let the family go, please," Jesus begged. He had already promised the family that he would let them go. Now here Omar was telling him that he had to kill them.

"They can identify you, and you can identify me. It's just way too risky," Omar explained. "The family has to go!"

"But, Omar . . ."

"No buts!" Omar snapped. "Either you kill the family or I'm going to have all you motherfuckers killed! You got 'til midnight to get this done. Now get the fuck out of my truck," he said in a dismissive tone.

thirty-four

Jesus got back behind the wheel of the car and pulled out into traffic. He had a big decision to make, and he wasn't sure if he was going to be able to do it. Keyon had done everything he had asked of him, and now Omar wanted Jesus to kill him as well as his wife and daughter.

"How did it go back there?" Keyon asked.

"Everything went good," Jesus lied. He didn't have the heart to tell Keyon about what was discussed inside Omar's truck.

"So now that you're out of the game, what's the plan for you?"

Jesus shrugged. "Haven't really had a chance to give it much thought yet, but I'm pretty sure I'll figure it out."

"So what's going on with you and Monica?" Keyon asked.

"What you mean?" Jesus asked with a confused look on his face.

"I see the way she looks at you, and I know you see it too," Keyon pointed out.

Jesus smiled. "Me and Monica never crossed that line. I used to date her sister before she died."

"Well I'm telling you that she has a thing for you," Keyon told him. "She seems like a good girl. Maybe you should give it a shot."

"I'll think about it," Jesus said as he pulled the car over to the side of the road. "Be right back. I gotta take a leak real quick." Jesus stepped out of the car and walked over to the woods. Jesus had his back turned to the car so Keyon couldn't see him. It looked as if Jesus was taking a leak, but he really pulled his gun from out of his crotch area, discreetly cocking a round into the chamber. He didn't want to kill Keyon, but Omar was leaving him with no choice. Jesus took a deep breath, and just as he was about to turn around and shoot Keyon he had a change of heart. His heart wouldn't allow him to murder Keyon, especially after all the stuff Keyon had done to help him come up with the money.

Jesus got back in the car and quickly pulled back

out into traffic.

***

Back at the room, Sabrina lay across the bed staring up at the ceiling with a smile on her face. She had been thanking God all day for answering her prayer and bringing her husband back to her in one piece. Sabrina couldn't wait to get back to her regular life. She had so many things to do as well as people to call. Her friends and family knew she and her family were going on a road trip, so they probably figured she wasn't answering her phone before because she was either busy or having too much fun to be worried about a stupid phone.

Another thing on Sabrina's to-do list was to help Mya get over the death of her boyfriend, Marcus. She wanted to help her get back to her normal life. Sabrina knew it would be rough, but she was up for the challenge. Sabrina's attention went straight to the front door when she heard it open and saw Keyon walk in holding a bottle of wine in his hand.

WRONG PLACE WRONG TIME

"We did it, baby. We finally free!" Keyon said in an excited tone. He pulled out several cups and placed them on the table and began pouring everyone a drink.

Monica looked up and noticed Jesus had a sour look on his face. She walked over and stood next to Jesus. "What's wrong?" she asked.

"Omar said he wants me to kill Keyon and his family, and if I don't he's going to kill all of us," Jesus whispered.

"For what? They haven't even done anything." Monica shook her head in disgust. She couldn't believe the outrageous request that Omar made. "So what are you going to do?"

Jesus shrugged. "I don't know yet. He said I have until midnight to get it done."

Keyon downed his first cup of wine and then quickly poured him another one. "Hey, why all the long faces over there?"

Jesus pulled his gun from his waistband and aimed it at Keyon's chest. "Omar said I have to kill you and your family or else he's going to have all of us killed."

Keyon sat his cup down and walked toward Jesus. "While we was in that car you told me if a man doesn't keep his word then that man is not a real man, and you gave me your word as a man," Keyon reminded him. After all the stuff he and his family had been through there was no way he was going out like this.

"Please don't do this," Sabrina said, standing behind her husband. "We've done everything you guys have asked of us."

Jesus stood there for a second and then lowered his weapon. He turned, dug down into his duffle bag, and pulled out three large stacks of cash and handed them to Keyon. "A real man always keeps his word."

Keyon took a step closer and hugged Jesus tightly. "Thank you," he whispered in Jesus's ear. Keyon grabbed his wife's and daughter's hand and led them out of the front door.

"Hey, Keyon!" Jesus called out, causing Keyon to stop in his tracks. "You take care of yourself."

Keyon smiled. "You do the same." And just like

that Keyon and his family were free at last.

Inside the car Keyon, Sabrina, and Mya celebrated. All three of them couldn't wait to get home and just lie in their own beds. They missed the little things like going in the refrigerator, turning the lights off and on, and sleeping in their own beds.

"Dad, can you please promise me one thing," Mya said from the backseat. "Promise me no more family reunions," she said as everyone in the car burst out in laughter.

thirty-five

*J*esus lay on the bed staring up at the ceiling. He asked himself over a hundred times if he had done the right thing by letting Keyon and his family go. Killing Keyon just didn't feel like the right thing to do in his heart.

"I know you not over here still thinking about that Keyon thing?" Monica asked as she lay down next to him. "You did the right thing. Fuck Omar."

"I've been doing some thinking," Jesus said. "Let's move to Mexico."

"Mexico?" Monica echoed. "Why Mexico?"

Jesus shrugged. "I don't know. Just thought new scenery might do us some good."

"Can we go to California?" Monica asked.

"Yes, of course," Jesus said with a smile. "I was also thinking when we move maybe we can get a place together," he said, throwing it out there.

"A place together meaning like you and me in the same house?" Monica asked, looking up into Jesus's eyes.

Jesus nodded. "Yes, that's what I'm asking you."

Monica leaned up and kissed Jesus on the lips. Jesus grabbed Monica, pulling her on top of him as he palmed her butt cheeks as the two continued to kiss. "You don't know how long I've been waiting for this," Monica said in between kisses. Jesus unbuckled Monica's pants, and then stopped.

"What's wrong?" Monica asked, breathing heavily. She was hoping that Jesus wasn't stopping because he was getting cold feet.

"Shhhh!" Jesus said as he sat completely still, listening. "You heard that?"

"Heard what?" Monica asked with a confused look on her face.

Jesus quickly pushed Monica off the bed and down to the floor. Then he hurriedly reached down and grabbed his machine gun from the foot of the bed as the front door busted open and two men entered the room.

Jesus quickly gunned the two men down before they could fully get inside the room. Jesus saw another gunman's arm peek around the corner and open fire inside the room. Jesus quickly dove over the bed to avoid getting hit with a blind bullet. Jesus kept his back close to the wall as he crept closer to the door. Once the gunfire stopped Jesus sprang from around the corner and shot the gunman in the neck. Jesus peeked out the door and saw that the coast was clear.

"Come on, Monica, we have to go!" Jesus said in a panic as he rushed and grabbed the duffle bag that contained the money. "Come on, we have to . . ." Jesus's words got caught in his throat when he looked over and saw Monica's eyes wide open with a small bullet hole in the center of her forehead.

Jesus melted down to his knees as the tears rolled down his face. He couldn't believe what he was seeing right now. Jesus looked down at his watch and the time read 11:25 p.m. Omar hadn't even given Jesus the full midnight deadline like he had promised. "I love you, baby," Jesus whispered as he grabbed the duffle bag and exited the motel room.

thirty-six

*K*eyon lay on his bed staring up at the ceiling with his arms folded behind his head. A part of him couldn't believe that he was a free man lying in his own bed. Sometimes his reality felt like a dream. Keyon knew it would take him some time to get back to normal, especially mentally. Since he'd been back home, Keyon hadn't found the time to have a discussion with Mya about everything that took place in the past week. He didn't want to just jump right into it, so Keyon decided to give Mya a little bit more time before bringing up such a sensitive topic.

Sabrina entered the room and spotted Keyon lying across the bed. "What you in here thinking about, baby?"

"A lot of things," Keyon said honestly. He felt bad that his family had to go through all the stuff they went through. If he could make it all go away he would.

Sabrina straddled her husband and planted soft kisses on his lips. "I just wanted to come in here and tell you thank you for everything you did for your family. We really appreciate it."

"Yeah right, you was probably hoping I didn't make it back," Keyon joked.

"Yeah right, there were a few times when I was about to go out looking for you myself," Sabrina laughed. "But seriously, I just wanted to say thank you. I know you may have had to do some not-so-godly things, but I'm just happy I have a husband willing to do those things for me. Thank you."

"Don't mention it, baby. I know you would have done the same for me." Keyon smiled as he sat up on the bed.

"Where you going, baby?" Sabrina asked.

"I think it's time I had a talk with Mya. I've been holding it off long enough," Keyon said as he exited his bedroom and walked down the hall toward Mya's room. Keyon took a deep breath and knocked on the door.

"Who is it?" Mya's voice called from the other

side of the door.

"It's me," Keyon answered. "May I come in?"

"Sure."

Keyon entered the room and saw Mya lying across her bed looking at something on her iPad. "You got a second to talk to your old man?"

"I guess," Mya said with a smile. "What do you want, Dad?"

"Just wanted to see how you were doing and how you were holding up," Keyon said feeling his daughter out. He knew she was trying to play it cool on the outside, but he wanted to find out what was going on with her on the inside.

"I been good," Mya replied. She knew this talk was coming, so she figured they might as well get it over with now. "What you want to talk about?"

"Just wanted to see how you were holding up," Keyon began. "And also I wanted to tell you how sorry I am about Marcus." Keyon didn't really care for Marcus, but at the same time he didn't want to kill him either.

"It's okay, Dad. I know you had to do what you

had to do," Mya said. "I was there, remember? I know you didn't have a choice."

Keyon smiled. "Thank you for forgiving me. It really means a lot to me because I know how much you liked Marcus."

"It's okay, Dad, I get it. We were just at the wrong place at the wrong time," Mya said in an understanding tone.

"Can I have a hug?" Keyon said with his arms outstretched. Mya leaned in and gave her dad a big hug. While the two were hugging, Keyon could hear Mya crying while her head was buried in his chest. "I love you, baby. Don't you ever forget that."

thirty-seven

*J*esus sat behind the wheel of another stolen car while R&B music hummed softly through the speakers at a low level. A part of him still couldn't believe Monica was dead. It was like the more Jesus tried not to think about it the more his brain thought about it, it was weird. Jesus wanted to go pay Omar a visit and get some revenge, but he knew there was no way he could stand up against Omar's army all by himself. That would be like bringing a knife to a gun fight. From the day he met Omar, Jesus knew he was bad news. In the midst of trying to get the money to pay Omar back, Jesus had lost his entire team. If Jesus could go back in time he would have definitely done things way differently. On the bright side, Jesus had a bag full of cash and his whole life ahead of him. Jesus had no choice but to start all over from scratch. It may take him a couple of years to get over the pain and losses he took, but at least he was still alive. As Jesus drove he couldn't help but wonder what Keyon and his family were doing at the moment. In another life Jesus wouldn't have minded being friends with Keyon. He was a stand-up guy, and Jesus respected anyone that was willing to do what he did for his family. In Jesus's book, Keyon was what you called a "real" man.

Jesus pulled the stolen car into the Greyhound parking lot and killed the engine. He was on his way to California to start a new life all by himself. At first he was going to take a plane like a normal person, but he figured it would be better to take the bus instead. The bus was more low key, not to mention he wouldn't have a problem getting his money on the bus. Jesus removed all his weapons, wiped them down, and tossed them into the backseat. Once that was done, he grabbed his duffle bag and headed inside the station. He walked through the station, and it felt like all eyes were on him. Jesus felt a little paranoid because he knew what he carried inside the duffle bag. He reached the counter, and a woman with red hair assisted him.

"Yes, how can I help you today?" the redhead

asked.

"Yes, can I get a one-way ticket to California, please?" Jesus smiled as he exchanged money for the ticket.

"Here you go, sweety." The redhead smiled. "You will be leaving out of gate 12 in an hour. Enjoy your trip."

"Thank you," Jesus said politely as he walked over and helped himself to a seat. He looked around at some of the people who waited to board other buses, and counted his blessings. As Jesus sat waiting to board his bus, he pulled out his phone and began googling some nice places in California. He didn't know anyone out there, nor did he know how to get around. He would have to figure all that out when he got there. Jesus stood to his feet and headed to the restroom. He stepped in the restroom, and the inside was cleaner than he expected. Jesus sat his bag down and relieved himself. He then walked over to the sink and popped two Tylenols into his mouth and swallowed them dry.

Jesus stood washing his hands, when he heard

one of the stall doors open and saw in the mirror a big man stepping out holding a shotgun in his hands. Instinctively Jesus spun around and reached for the gun on his waistband, only to remember he had left it in the car.

The big man stood and just looked at Jesus for a second. "Say goodnight, motherfucker!" he growled, and then pulled the trigger, blowing Jesus's head clean off his shoulders. The big man quickly stepped over Jesus's dead body and walked out of the restroom as if nothing had ever happened.

thirty-eight

*K*eyon and Sabrina sat on the couch enjoying a good movie. It felt good for the two to get back to doing normal things. Sabrina yawned and stretched her legs and then placed them in Keyon's lap. "I'm hungry. You want to go out and get something to eat?"

"What did you have in mind?" Keyon asked.

"Um, I don't know. Maybe seafood."

"Why? Because every time you see food you want to eat it?" That joke earned him a slap in the head with a pillow.

"Ha, ha, very funny," Sabrina huffed. "Let's get out of the house tonight."

"Wherever you want to go is fine with me. I just have to jump in the shower and get dressed," Keyon said as they heard a loud knock at the door. Keyon looked over at Sabrina. "You expecting anyone?"

Sabrina shook her head. "Nah, I was about to ask you the same thing."

Keyon stood to his feet and walked over to the door. "Who is it?"

"Police, open up!"

Keyon slowly opened the door. "Yes, may I help you?"

"Are you Keyon Brown?" the officer asked.

"Yes, that's me. What's this all about?" Keyon asked with a confused look on his face.

"You're under arrest for the murder of a police officer!" the officer said as several cops bum-rushed Keyon's home, slammed him face-first on the floor, and handcuffed his hands behind his back.

"This has to be some kind of mistake. I didn't murder no cop!" Keyon said, showing some resistance.

"Well we found your ID at the scene of the crime!" the officer told him.

Keyon lay on the floor in deep thought. Then it dawned on him. That night when Jesus had murdered the police officer the officer had never given Keyon back his ID.

The officer roughly pulled Keyon up to his feet

and escorted him toward the door.

"Baby, get my lawyer on the phone!" Keyon yelled as he was escorted out of his home.

Sabrina quickly pulled out her cell phone and dialed the lawyer's number and gave the lawyer a brief summary of what was going on.

"Calm down and don't worry. I'll be at the station first thing in the morning and sort all of this nonsense out," the lawyer assured her. Sabrina hung up and headed outside to make sure no foul play was going on with her husband.

"I called the lawyer, baby. Don't worry about nothing!" Sabrina yelled loud enough so Keyon could hear her. "Don't worry, I'm going to take care of everything; I promise!"

Keyon sat in the backseat of the police car, with a defeated look on his face. After all the stuff he went through to save his family, here he was sitting in the backseat of a police car looking foolish. He looked on with pain in his eyes as he watched Sabrina standing outside crying her poor little eyes out. Keyon mouth the words "I love you" as the cop car pulled away. The sight of Sabrina running alongside the police car broke Keyon's heart and crushed him. For the rest of the ride to the precinct, Keyon lay his head back and closed his eyes. He had finally reached an all-time low in his life.

"We going to show you how we deal with cop killers once we get you inside!" the driver of the cop car said in a serious tone with a no-nonsense look on his face. The police had no tolerance or respect for cop killers, and they planned on showing Keyon first-hand how they dealt with scum like him. When the cop car pulled up, Keyon could see all of the officers gathered around out front awaiting his arrival.

"Sir, I know you think I murdered your fellow officer, but I can assure you that this is a mistake," Keyon said from the backseat.

"Don't get scared now!" the officer barked as he roughly snatched Keyon out of the car. "Come on and take your punishment like a man!"

FIVE MONTHS LATER

Sabrina walked down the long corridor and stopped when she saw Keyon sitting behind glass sporting an orange jumpsuit. Sabrina sat down, picked up the phone, and placed it to her ear. "How you been holding up?

"I'm still alive," Keyon replied in a dry tone. Prison had really broken his spirit. "How have you been holding up?"

"I'm leaving you, Keyon," Sabrina said, looking down at the floor. "I can't do this jail relationship thing no more, I just can't."

"Why are you doing this to me?" Keyon asked, not believing his ears.

"Keyon, you have life in prison. What am I supposed to do with that? Huh? I have needs you know," Sabrina spat.

"I don't know if you forgot, but I'm sitting in here so that my family could still be alive and not six feet deep in someone's grave," he reminded her.

"So what am I supposed to do, pay you back

forever? I'm confused," Sabrina said, looking at Keyon with a disgusted look on her face. The last five months coming back and forth to visit Keyon had been horrible, not to mention she was now low on cash.

"Where's Mya?" Keyon asked. "I wrote her a few letters, and I never heard back from her."

"I haven't seen or heard from Mya in over a month. She met some new man and ran off with him." Sabrina shrugged as if it were no big deal.

"Why are you acting so cold like this?" Keyon couldn't believe his eyes nor what he was hearing.

"Listen, I just came up here to let you know that you were never going to see me again," Sabrina said, cutting straight to the chase. "I got a new man now. A real man," she said letting the words roll off of her tongue. "A better man than you'll ever be."

Keyon said nothing.

"Oh, and please stop writing me those tired-ass letters because I never read them. They just go straight into the trash where they belong." She was sick of checking mail and seeing Keyon's name on the front of the envelope. "Maybe while you're in here you can find yourself a new lover," she said with a devilish smirk on her face.

"You need to find your daughter and stop acting stupid," Keyon growled, trying to control his anger. He so badly wanted to reach through the glass and strangle Sabrina. Here he was sitting in jail for the rest of his life, and she thought it was funny. "What is this, some type of game to you? You treating me like this makes you feel good about yourself? All the shit I've done for this family, and you come up here and tell me this?"

"Fuck you and your daughter." Sabrina looked down at her watch. "Look, it's time for me to go, but before I do, I want you to say hi to my new man."

Keyon couldn't believe his eyes when he saw Omar sit down and pick up the phone.

"How's it going in there, Keyon?" Omar asked with a smile. "I hope it ain't no hard feelings, but I think I'm the better man for Sabrina. She needs someone who can be there for her and knows just how to 'handle' a woman like that, if you know what

I mean."

"You bastard! You and her had this whole thing planned from the jump, didn't you?" Keyon fumed. He felt like an idiot on the inside. Here he was doing any and everything he could to save his family, and come to find out his own wife had been against him from day one. Keyon felt like he was dreaming, but the sad part about it was this was no dream, but instead this was his reality.

"This ain't nothing personal, Keyon. You was just at the wrong place at the wrong time!" Omar said, and then hung up the phone. Keyon had no choice but to watch his wife leave with another man.

"Arghhh!" Keyon yelled as he banged the phone repeatedly on the glass until a couple of COs rough detained him and took him away to the box.

THE END

Text Good2Go at 31996 to receive new release updates via text message

BOOKS BY GOOD2GO AUTHORS

SILK WHITE — **SILK WHITE** — **JACOB SPEARS** — **JACOB SPEARS** — **SILK WHITE**

ERNEST MORRIS — **MYCHEA** — **MYCHEA** — **MYCHEA**

MYCHEA — **MYCHEA** — **ERNEST MORRIS** — **SILK WHITE** — **ASIA HILL**

ASIA HILL — **MYCHEA** — — **SILK WHITE** — **SILK WHITE**

SLUMPED PART 1
JASON BRENT

A TALE BY SILK WHITE
STRANDED

TEARS OF A HUSTLER
A NOVEL BY SILK WHITE

TEARS OF A HUSTLER 2
A NOVEL BY SILK WHITE

TEARS OF A HUSTLER 3
A NOVEL BY SILK WHITE

TEARS OF A HUSTLER
YOU'VE BEEN WARNED
A NOVEL BY SILK WHITE

A NOVEL BY SILK WHITE
TEARS OF A HUSTLER 5
THE SPADES

SILK WHITE
TEARS OF A HUSTLER 6

THE TEFLON QUEEN
A NOVEL BY SILK WHITE

THE TEFLON QUEEN 2
A NOVEL BY SILK WHITE

THE TEFLON QUEEN 3
SILK WHITE

THE TEFLON QUEEN 4
SILK WHITE

THE TEFLON QUEEN 5
DEEP COVER
SILK WHITE

THE TEFLON QUEEN
NO MERCY
SILK WHITE

THE PANTY RIPPER
REALITY WAY

THE PANTY RIPPER 3
REALITY WAY

TIED TO A BOSS
J.L. ROSE

TIME IS MONEY

YOUNG GOONZ
REALITY WAY

**THE HAND I WAS DEALT WEB SERIES
NOW AVAILABLE ON YOUTUBE!**

**SEASON TWO NOW AVAILABLE
NOW AVAILABLE ON YOUTUBE!**

**THE HACKMAN
NOW AVAILABLE ON YOUTUBE!**

To order books, please fill out the order form below:
To order films please go to **www.good2gofilms.com**

Name:_____

Address:_____

City: _____ State: _____ Zip Code: _____

Phone:_____

Email:_____

Method of Payment: Check   VISA   MASTERCARD

Credit Card#:_____

Name as it appears on card: _____

Signature: _____

Item Name	Price	Qty	Amount
48 Hours to Die – Silk White	$14.99		
A Hustler's Dream - Ernest Morris	$14.99		
A Hustler's Dream 2 - Ernest Morris	$14.99		
Bloody Mayhem Down South	$14.99		
Business Is Business – Silk White	$14.99		
Business Is Business 2 – Silk White	$14.99		
Business Is Business 3 – Silk White	$14.99		
Childhood Sweethearts – Jacob Spears	$14.99		
Childhood Sweethearts 2 – Jacob Spears	$14.99		
Childhood Sweethearts 3 - Jacob Spears	$14.99		
Childhood Sweethearts 4 - Jacob Spears	$14.99		
Flipping Numbers – Ernest Morris	$14.99		
Flipping Numbers 2 – Ernest Morris	$14.99		
He Loves Me, He Loves You Not - Mychea	$14.99		
He Loves Me, He Loves You Not 2 - Mychea	$14.99		
He Loves Me, He Loves You Not 3 - Mychea	$14.99		
He Loves Me, He Loves You Not 4 – Mychea	$14.99		
He Loves Me, He Loves You Not 5 – Mychea	$14.99		
Lord of My Land – Jay Morrison	$14.99		
Lost and Turned Out – Ernest Morris	$14.99		
Married To Da Streets – Silk White	$14.99		
M.E.R.C. - Make Every Rep Count Health and Fitness	$14.99		
My Besties – Asia Hill	$14.99		
My Besties 2 – Asia Hill	$14.99		
My Besties 3 – Asia Hill	$14.99		
My Besties 4 – Asia Hill	$14.99		
My Boyfriend's Wife - Mychea	$14.99		
My Boyfriend's Wife 2 – Mychea	$14.99		
Naughty Housewives – Ernest Morris	$14.99		
Naughty Housewives 2 – Ernest Morris	$14.99		
Naughty Housewives 3 – Ernest Morris	$14.99		
Naughty Housewives 4 – Ernest Morris	$14.99		

Never Be The Same – Silk White	$14.99		
Stranded – Silk White	$14.99		
Slumped – Jason Brent	$14.99		
Tears of a Hustler - Silk White	$14.99		
Tears of a Hustler 2 - Silk White	$14.99		
Tears of a Hustler 3 - Silk White	$14.99		
Tears of a Hustler 4- Silk White	$14.99		
Tears of a Hustler 5 – Silk White	$14.99		
Tears of a Hustler 6 – Silk White	$14.99		
The Panty Ripper - Reality Way	$14.99		
The Panty Ripper 3 – Reality Way	$14.99		
The Solution – Jay Morrison	$14.99		
The Teflon Queen – Silk White	$14.99		
The Teflon Queen 2 – Silk White	$14.99		
The Teflon Queen 3 – Silk White	$14.99		
The Teflon Queen 4 – Silk White	$14.99		
The Teflon Queen 5 – Silk White	$14.99		
The Teflon Queen 6 - Silk White	$14.99		
The Vacation – Silk White	$14.99		
Tied To A Boss - J.L. Rose	$14.99		
Tied To A Boss 2 - J.L. Rose	$14.99		
Tied To A Boss 3 - J.L. Rose	$14.99		
Tied To A Boss 4 - J.L. Rose	$14.99		
Time Is Money - Silk White	$14.99		
Two Mask One Heart – Jacob Spears and Trayvon Jackson	$14.99		
Two Mask One Heart 2 – Jacob Spears and Trayvon Jackson	$14.99		
Two Mask One Heart 3 – Jacob Spears and Trayvon Jackson	$14.99		
Wrong Place Wrong Time	$14.99		
Young Goonz – Reality Way	$14.99		
Young Legend – J.L. Rose	$14.99		
Subtotal:			
Tax:			
Shipping (Free) U.S. Media Mail:			
Total:			

Make Checks Payable To:
Good2Go Publishing
7311 W Glass Lane,
Laveen, AZ 85339